I0831147

ARMAGEDDON
WAS
QUIET

BY

MIKE L. BOWEN

Published by Mike L. Bowen

First Edition

Copyright © 2006 by Mike L. Bowen

All rights reserved. This book, or parts thereof, may not be reproduced in any form without permission.

ISBN 978-0-6151-3644-8

All the characters in this book are fictitious, and any resemblance to actual persons, living or dead, is purely coincidental.

Dedicated to my wife Stella for putting up with me during the writing of this book.

From The New Testament

Revised New American Bible

The Book of Revelation to John

Chapter 16: 14b-18

16:14b ...They went out to the kings of the whole world to assemble them for the battle on the great day of God the almighty.

16:15 "Behold, I am coming like a thief." Blessed is the one who watches and keeps his clothes ready, so that he may not go naked and people see him exposed.

16:16 They then assembled the kings in the place that is named Armageddon in Hebrew.

16:17 The seventh angel poured out his bowl into the air. A loud voice came out of the temple from the throne, saying, "It is done."

16:18 Then there were lightning flashes, rumblings, and peals of thunder, and a great earthquake. It was such a violent earthquake that there has never been one like it since the human race began on earth.

Chapter 1

The day is hot but not depressingly so. A cool breeze drifts over the hill from the bay area keeping the heat from rising above record-breaking proportions. The weatherman promises it will be a little bit cooler tomorrow. A few degrees won't make much of a difference. It's been hotter then the seasonal average for over a week. Kids open fire hydrants on street corners and jump into fountains at the city plaza. Going to work or school under these intolerable conditions is uncomfortable but most manage the best they can while others simply play hooky.

Those who work indoors take fewer trips outside and more trips to the water cooler. Those working outdoors envy the ones inside and bring their water bottles with them. It's not so bad if your work situation allows you to keep the water cold in an ice chest for drinking and pouring over your body to cool you down like the construction workers putting up the new bank building on the corner of Second and Elm. Not everyone is so lucky. Climbing down from their garbage truck at the end of the days run Antonio wipes the sweat from his brow with the back of his right wrist and turns to his partner Pat.

"It keeps up like this and I'm going to look for another job inside somewhere, like in a meat cooler. Or better yet, a nice cool office behind a desk. I mean its not even summer yet for Christ's sake." He doesn't sound convincing. He'd never work indoors no matter what the temperature outside or the job inside.

Pat snickers, "Yea, right. You love the smell of garbage in all this heat. It's what you live for."

"Yea, well, it smells better than you. What's that after shave of yours, Ode 'de Ripe Tomato?" replies Antonio.

"Up yours. Besides, you wouldn't know what to do with yourself sitting at a desk anyway. You'd end up sittin' in the chair playing with yourself. Come on, let's go sign out." Pat heads for the shack ahead of Antonio still chuckling at the thought of him sitting behind a desk buried in a pile of paperwork. It would be like he died and went straight to hell. Pat knows because he would feel exactly the same way if it happened to him. Heaven forbid.

Antonio catches up with Pat, slaps him hard on the back of his shoulder. "So, you got anybody lined up for the weekend?" Antonio inquires. Pat knows whatever answer he gives there will be some kind of sarcastic comeback. He can't live down his reputation for being a ladies man, a most eligible bachelor, and renowned playboy of the Tri-valley area. He remembers how it was before Antonio and Maria got married when the three of them searched the clubs almost every Friday and Saturday night for the right girl for Pat. Sometimes they found a girl, sometimes not, but never anyone you could call right. There was even talk as to whether such a girl possibly existed.

Pat just tried to be cool about it saying, "Naw, things are kinda thin right now. Ain't exactly seeing anyone in particular you know. That's just not my style."

"You don't have any style Pat. That's part of your problem. If the girls are thinned out, it's because you just kinda used them all up, and there just ain't nobody left. Words got around, 'stay away from Pat the pervert. He's no good.' You need to find new territory dude, someplace where they never heard of you. Know what I mean?"

"Up yours, Antonio," Pat said.

They climbed the short staircase into the shack where Guido was sitting on high backless stool, cigarette over his left ear, pencil in his right hand, and some of his lunch still on the front of his shirt. Their boss, a large rotund Italian, looks like he's had more than his fair share of pasta. This of course embarrasses Antonio to think they might have come from the same stock. He was proud of his Italian heritage and was sensitive about things that put it in a poor light. Including Guido. His father always told him to be proud of who he was and where he came from. He took pride in being an American but he appreciated his Italian ancestry. Antonio took it serious. The only thing Guido took seriously was food.

Pat goes to the time book and purposely signs out slowly making Antonio wait impatiently. He knows Antonio has little patience and this always pisses him off. Pat frequently makes a point of getting to the log first just for this purpose. Antonio finally gives Pat a shove and grabs the pen out of his hand.

"Give me that you jerk," he said with false bravado.

Pat laughs and gives Antonio a friendly shove back as he heads for the door, "Later, Guido," he says on his way out.

Guido snorts in his usual 'I don't give a shit' manner and reminds Pat, "Watch out pullin' outa the yard you don't kill someone. I mean it this time Patrick." Guido knows he hates to be called Patrick and puts exaggerated emphasis on the name as he gives Pat the same warning he gives every day, and Pat ignores just as often. Pat's usual habit of pulling out of the dirt parking area kicking up dust in the summer and mud in the winter is a constant aggravation for Guido. Pat knows it and that just encourages him all the more.

Antonio tosses the pen to the next guy signing out and follows Pat out the door telling Guido on the way, "Hey, man, don't worry about it. He's just showing off. Maybe one of these days he'll grow up, get a real job, and surprise us all." He closes the door behind him and climbs down the steps.

Pat hollers back over his shoulder, feigning hurt and injury, "I thought you were my friend. You're supposed back me up."

"Hey, man. Just trying to help," says Antonio laughing and shrugging his shoulders.

They head for Pat's '72 Mustang in the employee parking area. He got the car from his favorite uncle for his 16th birthday and it remains his pride and joy. His uncle died during the last days of the Vietnam War and Pat keeps the car as his only tangible link to a man he loved and respected more than his own father. Uncle Michael O'Conner was more of a father figure to him than was his dad. Even though they were brothers Pat's dad and uncle couldn't have been more different in temperament and personality. Mike and Don O'Conner grew up in the Irish blue collar section of Boston and came out west when very young to get away from a hard working, hard drinking, and hard disciplinarian of a father who beat them and their mother more times than either cared to remember.

When Don married and started a family he tried hard not to be like his father. He wanted to be a better man than his dad, but hard times and a weak personality made life difficult for him to cope with. He came home late and drunk from work one night when Pat was too young to remember. After a short argument with Pat's pregnant mother over some minor episode and in a fit of drunken rage Don hit her harder then he meant, but hard enough that she lost the baby. The guilt he felt from what he did never left him no matter how much he tried to drink it away. He never touched his wife or son again in anger, or affection.

Mike knew what his brother did was wrong but understood Don's faults and where they came from. As young Pat was growing up Mike tried to convince him not to be too hard on his father. Uncle Mike would take Pat fishing or for a hike in the near by hills while his dad would sit in front of the TV, often too drunk to follow the game he was supposed to be watching. His mother spent so much time wallowing in self-pity over her lot in life that she had little time to be a proper mother for young Pat. He grew up loving and hating her at the same time. He swore he would never end up like his parents. If that was what marriage did to people he would have none of it. He's never had an honest close relationship in his life. The thought of one scares the hell out of him.

It never ceases to amaze Antonio how Pat can peel out of the parking area in a billow of smoke and dust every day without sooner or later hitting someone while going through the gate. They have come close a couple of times and even started a fistfight on one occasion. The summer before last two boys in their early teens were barreling down the road on bicycles oblivious to anything around them racing to see who could get to little league practice first. It was a matter of honor and nothing was going to slow either one of them down. Both had bragged all day at school that they were the fastest cyclist in town and the whole team was waiting at the ball field to see who would get there first. Neither noticed the Mustang heading for the street as they approached the gate nor did Pat see them. Only Antonio's last second scream at Pat to slam on the brakes avoided a tragedy. Pat let out a stream of expletives but never mentioned the incident again. It scared him more than he wanted to admit.

One incident that Pat does mention, and often, happened about eight months ago when Pat was upset about being stood up for a date with Rosie, the cashier down at Parker Center Drug Store. He spent most of the day complaining about what he considered a grave put down till Antonio was ready to walk off and let Pat finish the route alone. When they pulled out of the lot at day's end Pat was still complaining and not paying attention to traffic. They cut off a car speeding by just as oblivious of them as Pat was of it. Words were exchanged and before it was over Pat and the other driver got out and started exchanging fists as well. Antonio was able to break it up before any one got hurt and everybody went on their way. To this day however, Pat insists he beat the crap out of the other guy but Antonio just shakes his head and keeps silent. Let Pat have his moment of glory.

"One of these days why don't you give Guido a heart attack and drive out of the lot in a slow and careful manner?" Antonio suggests. "Might surprise the shit out of everybody."

"What, and spoil my reputation? Why?" Pat exclaims. "Besides, if I give him enough grief maybe he'll retire early and then I'll get his job and not have to put up with you all day, every day. Sounds like a plan to me."

"You should be so lucky," Antonio laughs.

They head over to Ernie's Pool Hall as they do most days after work and stay till early evening. They shoot pool, and the breeze, cop a feel whenever Cindy, Ernie's only waitress, walks by, which is surprisingly more often than you would think under the circumstances, and generally waste away the afternoon. Ernie's is not exactly a family entertainment place despite the sign in the front window to the contrary, but they enjoy the macho atmosphere, Pat's occasional pool hustle, and the time spent together away from work and less than ideal home situations. What they don't know is Cindy has a mad crush on Pat, like most women long on body but short on brains.

She came to work at Ernie's about a year and a half ago. She was desperate for a job after being fired from her previous place of employment for not giving in to her boss's sexual advances. He was married and a slob and she had no interest in fooling around but he was persistent. She finally had enough and let him have it with a right cross and a knee in the groin one afternoon and he let her go. Her job skills were limited so finding work wasn't easy. Ernie put up a hard cold front but was a softy at heart and when Cindy came in begging for a job he couldn't refuse her.

He really didn't need a waitress but her good looks and pleasant personality helped bring in customers. He kept an eye on customers who got too friendly and made working conditions for her safe and comfortable. The pay wasn't great but the tips were good and she was content. Pat was the only one who could get away with being too friendly but Ernie knew him from a long way back and how Cindy felt about him. Pat was aware of her feelings also but never asked her out. He actually liked her more than he would let on and that's what scared him. He thought it might have a chance of getting too serious and he couldn't handle that.

Chapter 2

When Pat and Antonio leave the pool hall and go their separate ways they go to homes and lives as different as their personalities. While they share a bond of friendship and camaraderie that comes from years of school, sports, work, and carousing together, they also have different dreams and expectations of what their future should hold. Antonio is married, has two kids, a boy and a girl. Maria was his high school sweetheart. There hasn't really been anyone else for either one of them.

They saw each other around campus from time to time during their sophomore year, but didn't really meet and get to know each other until they were juniors. From then on it was like they were magnets. It was like they were glued together. They were inseparable. By the middle of their senior year it was taken for granted by all their friends that wedding bells would ring sometime after high school. Antonio hadn't actually popped the question yet, but some of their friends were taking bets on when that would happen. It happened on graduation night.

The wedding didn't take place right away. They wanted some time to plan and make decisions on what they were going to do and where they wanted to go with their lives. They both made a gallant attempt at furthering their education at the local junior college, but while neither was academically challenged, they were not exactly what you would call academically gifted either. They dropped out of college during their second semester and married a few months later.

Even their parents were excited about what everyone considered a good match. Neither family was well off so they chipped in together to give the kids the biggest and best wedding possible. Everything went smoothly and even the weather cooperated. The bride was beautiful, the ceremony was emotionally magnificent, the reception was marvelous, both the food and the dancing. They honeymooned along the Monterey coast for almost a week where everything seemed magical and heavenly.

When the week ended they reluctantly headed home but looked forward to starting their life together. They had high hopes and great expectations, but they were young, maybe too young. It didn't take long for the reality of married life to hit them. Maria soon became pregnant with Theresa and once she was born their whole lifestyle changed. Maria wrapped herself in the new role of both wife and mother and struggled with the changes. While Antonio was proud to be a new father, he wasn't sure about his new role and became confused and uncertain of himself. Maria seemed to him to become more distant. He didn't understand her new responsibilities and wasn't too clear about his.

A gap seemed to come between them that they never fully recovered from though they have tried each in their own way. While they are not really happy you couldn't say they're unhappy either. They loved each other and their daughter. When Ryan was born their difficulties magnified themselves a little. There was a communication problem concerning the needs and desires each had for themselves and each other. Try they did but just couldn't seem to find a solution.

Both seem to drift from day to day taking life as it comes without any meaning beyond the routine of housecleaning, cooking, sending kids to school, shopping, and for Antonio the repetition of emptying one overflowing garbage can after another, house to house, street to street, in an unending stream. They were raised in good Italian Catholic families and no matter how uncomfortable things got between them divorce never entered their minds. It just was not an option. They were in it for the long haul and both accepted that reality. They might have continued this way for the rest of their lives if it weren't for unexpected and unforeseen changes about to occur.

Pat on the other hand can't understand the relationship of Antonio and Maria, or any other married couple for that matter. The experience with his parents colors his perception of what family life is all about. There are times when he sees models of good family togetherness and joy and he wonders how it might have been if his parents had been more like that. In looking back he is more appreciative of what Uncle Mike did for him. Pat now believes that if it weren't for Uncle Mike he might have ended up a bitter hopeless person and maybe even headed for prison. Life is still not ideal. He knows he has relationship problems and may always have them. He is not only single, but expects that to be a life long condition. The idea of settling down with one woman for more then a weekend is as alien to him as divorce is to Antonio and Maria.

Antonio takes the bus from Ernie's. They decided early on that they could save a lot of money if they kept to one car for Maria to use during the day and he would take the bus to and from work. He didn't have far to go and the bus stop was right on the corner and dropped him off right in front of the yard where he worked. It was the same coming home from the pool hall and Pat frequently gave him a ride home though not every day. He usually arrives home around 5:30 but never later than six.

The bus ride is almost always uneventful and he finds time to observe people as they get on and off the bus. He finds this much more enjoyable than reading the newspaper as the news is always depressing. Antonio was surprised when he first started riding the bus to find fewer regular riders than he expected. He originally thought he would find someone he would sit with after striking up a friendship and have someone to talk with on a regular basis to or from work if not both ways. It didn't work out that way much to his dismay. What he sees a lot of are the old ladies who apologize for their slowness getting on, and the old men who expect everyone else to wait for them because their speed isn't what it use to be. There are also the late shopping wives who spent too much money and time in the stores now in a hurry to get home to make dinner, and the smart-ass teenagers looking for trouble instead of staying home to do their homework. The latter bothers him the most because he sees a lot of himself in them, though he would never admit it.

The bus stops about a half a block from his apartment. As he walks up the steps to his front door he can hear Maria screaming at one of the kids and he wonders aloud, "Good Lord, now what? Can't that woman ever stop screaming?" He opens the door and enters the parlor. He always thought it was a living room, but Maria insists on calling it the parlor. She says it sounds more elegant and as long as they live in a complex that outwardly is a little more posh in appearance than your average apartment building she wants to bring the same atmosphere inside the apartment as well.

Maria is crossing the parlor heading for the kitchen. Without pausing or looking his way she says sarcastically, "How's Cindy feeling these days, or have you started groping for Pat now?"

Antonio sighs, "Can it, woman. What's for dinner?"

"You better have a talk with Theresa. She's had a bad day. Something at school but I can't get it out of her. She's been in her room since she got home. She won't talk to me." Maria stopped at the stove and checked the pot of boiling spaghetti. It must be Wednesday Antonio thought. Wednesday is spaghetti night. It's the same routine every week. It never varies. It did have its advantages. At least he never really had to question what was for dinner on any given night except for Saturday. That was surprise night. It mostly consisted of the week's leftovers unless there was some special occasion.

As Antonio heads for Theresa's room Maria hollers, "Give Ryan a spanking. He's done it again." He knows what that means. First things first though. He walks into his daughter's bedroom and sees her lying on her bed reading a book, or at least pretending to. It's obvious she is not really into the book, as her eyes appear more focused miles away than on the words of the page. Her eyes look slightly red and puffy like she has been crying. Several crumpled tissues lie on the bed near her book.

Seeing his daughter like this gives him some pangs of guilt as he realizes more and more lately that he has not really gotten into his children's lives. He has not been there for their little triumphs at school like Theresa's starring role in the Christmas pageant, or when she won second place in the school spelling bee. Ryan wants to start little league this year but Antonio has been making excuses why he can't join his son in the activities that the league wants fathers to participate. His usual excuse is his job and the hours he must keep. He wants to be a good father, but he just doesn't know how. He has made up his mind to do better but he doesn't know when or where to start. He walks over and sits down on the edge of her bed putting his hand on her shoulder giving it a little squeeze.

"Hi, Pumpkin. How's daddy's girl? Your mom says you ain't feelin' so hot." She turned in his direction but wouldn't look him in the eye.

She gave a little half-hearted shrug and said, "It's nothing."

Obviously it was something and she was trying to put up a brave little front. Antonio felt for her. He knew how much he loved his daughter and wanted to help her, but just hoped whatever the problem; it wasn't some girl thing that needed mom's help more than dad's.

"It's something if my little Pumpkin locks herself in her room staring at a book she's not reading instead of watching TV, or riding her bike. Now trust me, I can't help you if I don't know what the problem is. I can't read your mind, so you'll just have to tell me what's bothering you. Then, maybe, if we put both our heads together, just maybe, we might come up with a solution."

"Daddy, you're not a girl. You wouldn't understand."

"No, I'm not a girl. And I'm really glad you noticed that," Antonio smiled and tried to take a light approach hoping to take some of the gloom and doom off the face of his little girl and out of the air. The fear that this might be a girl thing he couldn't handle just increased significantly. He pushed forward just the same hoping to be her knight in shining armor. "But that doesn't mean I don't understand. Try me."

She looked up at him not sure if this would work. How could she tell dad? Guys just don't understand she thought. But she decided to give it a try. After all, she couldn't tell mom. She didn't want to hurt mom's feelings. "You know that new dress mom made me, the green one?"

"Yes, I know the one."

"Well, I wore it to school today," she started and the dam broke. She let it all out glad to have someone to tell it to, "and Shelley and Debra laughed at me. They said it looked funny. They kept making fun of me until I was ready to punch them, but I didn't. You see why I couldn't tell mom. I was afraid it would hurt mom's feelings. I couldn't do that after all the work she put into making the dress for me."

"What do you think of the dress?" Antonio inquired. He wanted to know what she thought of the dress but he was also buying time to think of an answer to her problem. She got real excited now.

"I love it! I think it's beautiful, it's the best dress in the whole world, and mommy worked so hard to make it for me. I was proud to wear it to school until they started making fun of it."

"Did they know your mom made it for you?" he asked.

"Yea, I told them and that's when they started saying mean things about it. They said we couldn't afford to buy a dress like the fancy stores they go to at the mall."

Antonio knew where to go now. "Well, you know what I think?" She was looking down at her hands and shook her head. "I think they're just jealous."

She looked up at him quizzically, "Jealous?"

"Sure. Do their moms ever take the time to make them dresses?"

"No."

"Well, there you are. Look, honey, you can't go through life worrying about what other people think. I learned that lesson a long time ago. You just have to be yourself. You like the dress, right?"

"Yea."

"Then wear it whenever and wherever you want, and don't let what others think or say interfere with your enjoying wearing that dress or anything else you like. Be your own person. Show them that you wear what you want because you want to please yourself, not them. Be a leader, not a follower. Don't let them take something special away from you just because they don't have something special. Like I said, just be your self. You are somebody special and don't let anyone tell you different."

Theresa seemed to take in what he was saying. He could see the change in her face as he was talking and she appeared to come out of her depression and brighten up considerably. A big smile came across her face as she reached up and put her arms around his neck and hugged him tightly, "I love you, daddy. Thank you."

"I love you, too sweetheart."

Antonio left his daughter's room feeling good about himself and for Theresa. It was short lived however. He stared at the door to his son's room and realized that Ryan's situation was not quite the same. No one was picking on him. It was more like the other way around. Ryan had a habit of picking on the little boy down the street. The boys never got along ever since kindergarten though Antonio never really understood what started it, and Ryan being the bigger of the two constantly pushed the other boy around. Antonio figured boys need to work things out for themselves, but when the pushing got a little too much the other boy's mom complains to Maria and she leaves it up to Antonio to discipline Ryan.

He steps into Ryan's bedroom and the boy looks up expecting the worst. Antonio decides a spanking isn't what's required.

"You know that fishing trip we were planning in two weeks?"

Ryan looked up and felt his heart drop, "Yea." It was a trip they had been planning for several months now. Ryan was looking forward to it with great anticipation and thrilled at the prospect of catching his favorite fish to bring home for mom to cook. They were going bass fishing on a real boat and everything.

"Tomorrow you apologize to Brandon or you stay home and I will take your sister fishing with me."

Ryan almost died. His mouth dropped and his eyes opened wide. This was going to be worse than he thought. It would be bad enough to lose the fishing trip, but to have his sister take his place, that would be the biggest humiliation of all time. His parents always seemed to know how to push the right buttons. He couldn't understand it. It was almost like they could read his mind. As much as he hated the idea of saying he was sorry to that little brat Brandon, he knew he'd better do it.

Reluctantly he replied, "Yes, father."

"Oh, and I don't want to hear anymore of this in the next two weeks or you will still lose the trip. OK?"

"Yes, father." What was the world coming to Ryan wondered.

Antonio walks down the hall back to the kitchen where dinner is almost ready. Maria is setting the table. Whatever faults she may have, he was thinking, cooking isn't one of them. She's the best damn cook he ever met, except for his mother of course.

Chapter 3

After saying goodbye to Antonio, Pat hung around the pool hall trying to hustle up a money game but without any luck. Most of the regulars knew better and the few who didn't wouldn't be around for at least another hour. He left Ernie's and headed for his apartment fully intent on fixing himself some dinner, usually the frozen TV variety, and catching the game on TV. During baseball season he spent more time watching the Giants, either on TV or at Candlestick Park, then playing pool. He hated cold windy Candlestick Park and couldn't wait for the local yahoo's in the city to quit wrangling over their political differences and get the Giants a new downtown baseball stadium. He couldn't understand the local electorate in the City. They put into the office of mayor a known corrupt machine politician from the State Assembly, and seemed more hell bent on pleasing the local faggots than on working for the whole community. Pat really didn't think much of people in the City anyway. They didn't deserve the Giants.

He didn't have season tickets but he went to as many games as his time and budget would allow, which of course was never enough. While he had no problem going to a game by himself where he could concentrate all his attention and energy on the game, he much preferred going with a couple of the guys from work or from the pool hall. It was a macho guy thing, going to the ballpark sharing the game, the beer, the fun, the sun, and the stories of glory days gone by when they were the high school baseball heroes and the idle of all the starry eyed cheerleaders.

Pat even took an occasional date to a game, but she had to be a big Giants fan and had to know her baseball, or it was a useless wasted effort. He was an avid Giants fan, some would even say obsessive, and though it was the middle of the season he was a firm believer that every game counted. An early season loss in a close game would drive him up the wall, as he knew it would come back to haunt them in the late going come September. He rooted for a win just as hard the first week of the season as he did the last week of a tight pennant race. He was the kind of fan that every franchise owner dreams having more of.

Pat wasn't going to miss any more games than work, pool, or women would allow. The job rarely interfered with watching or going to a Giants game considering the hours they worked. A hot game of pool with money on the line did have its priority. He was a pretty fair pool player and could hustle with the best of them. Well enough in fact that he did supplement his income with several money games a week. Pat didn't mind missing one Giants game to earn enough playing pool to cover the cost of tickets for several games at a later time.

He always wanted to buy a season ticket but his income and lifestyle made that purchase a little too financially uncomfortable. Besides, if he had season tickets the times he went with a group of friends or a date they normally couldn't buy seats next to his, which meant if he wanted to sit next to them he would have to buy another ticket for himself, and that made no sense. Pat was happy pool hustling the money to buy seats as needed.

Antonio would watch and enjoy Pat's success hustling pool but would never play for money himself. He was good but not that good. He only played for the pure enjoyment of the game and let Pat take all the risks.

Not only was it more fun that way but it was also less stressful. Besides, as a single man Pat could afford to lose, although he would never admit it. Antonio didn't have that luxury. Somehow family obligations always seemed to require more and more financial investment, and luxury expenses like sports season tickets, or risks like losing while playing pool were simply out of the question.

Pat had a reputation as a lady's man and when it came to a woman versus a Giants game, well, that was a different story. It really depended on who she was, how much of a baseball fan she was, her knowledge of the game, and how she rated on a scale of ten. Pat thought of himself as being a bit old fashioned. He still believed in rating women on a scale of ten. A perfect woman, a ten, didn't really exist, no woman was that good in Pat's mind. But a nine came close, few of them as there were, and not only would she look good, but she would go to the game with him, or watch the game with him on TV, and then have sex afterwards. That was Pat's idea of a perfect relationship, as long as she didn't stay long, or try to get too serious. That just spoiled everything.

Pat stopped at the market on the way home to pick up a few things, he didn't feel like his usual frozen dinner tonight, so he decided to get some potato chips, hamburger for the Hibachi, and of course Miller High Life beer, a necessary item while watching any game. It wasn't that he thought Miller High Life was any better than any other beer, most of his buddies preferred Budweiser or Coors; he just liked the sound of it. 'Miller High Life', it just sounded cool to say, like it had more class. He wasn't a heavy drinker but he did like his beer. Memories of what booze did to his father and the effect that had on his mother, kept Pat from becoming a real boozer. While many of the guys bragged how fast they put down a six or twelve pack, Pat was content to let a twelve pack last a week or more.

Heavy drinkers put him off. They brought back too many bad memories. He's even been known to throw an obnoxious drunk out of his apartment during parties or other gatherings. Pat was well enough liked by everybody that he could get away with it. Friends surprisingly discovered they could have a good time, even a better time, without getting drunk. It actually added to Pat's popularity, especially among the women. That didn't bother him at all.

He pulled into the Lucky's shopping center and parked his Mustang near the exit doors taking up two parking spaces as usual. He didn't want anyone denting his pride and joy by opening their car door in total disregard of other people's property, especially his. Antonio always complained that he was just being selfish and hated people who took up two parking spaces especially when the lot was crowded, but Pat was adamant that he was only protecting something that was more important to him than most people could understand. Antonio knew what the car meant to Pat so he never really pushed the issue.

Picking up a shopping cart outside the entrance Pat went through the automatic doors, his mind preoccupied on the game, wondering if the team was going to be affected this year with its infamous June swoon. While he professed not to believe in the annual slide of his team discussed in the sports pages this time every year, it hung there in the back of his mind. He just hoped it wasn't hanging in the back of the player's minds. If they thought about it too much it could become a self-fulfilling prophecy.

Heading down the soap and bleach aisle he made a fast left turn at the end, around the display of a new breakfast cereal, ramming the cart of a reasonably attractive redhead and knocking down boxes of cereal across both aisles and bringing the attention of half the shoppers in the store directly upon them. The redhead jumped in shock and was brought abruptly out of her own preoccupation over the recent breakup with her boyfriend, the louse. She started to yell at the clumsy oaf who crashed into her cart but stopped short when she thought she recognized him.

"Pat?" she asked.

"Oh, shit. Sorry lady… Sue?" He recognized her as one of his weekend companions from sometime back but the details were a bit fuzzy now. They usually were past Wednesday of any given week. He never dwelt long on any of his weekend encounters for fear of the relationship developing into something more meaningful, which he could never risk. "What are you doing here?" Pat asked dumbly ignoring the obvious.

"Well, I was trying to shop," she said with a tease in her voice, "but some oaf who wasn't looking where he was going kind of held me up." She smiled.

"Hey, I'm real sorry. I just wasn't looking. Had something on my mind I guess." Pat was feeling sheepishly uncomfortable as he noticed several people still staring at him and the mess on the floor. Two stocking clerks were approaching them from opposite directions to clean it up in response to an announcement over the speaker system alerting the whole store to their predicament.

"So, what are you up to? It's been a while," Pat said, trying to put himself at ease and make things appear more normal. He didn't mind being the center of attention, but not this kind. He didn't handle embarrassment very well.

"It's been a while since you said you were going to call me," she reminded him. He always said he would call them but rarely ever did. It was his way of keeping things in perspective. No commitment was his motto, after all, wasn't variety the spice of life?

"You know how it is," he said shrugging his shoulders passing it off as no big deal. To him it never was. "One thing after another and time just has a way of flying by." He wished it would fly a little faster right at the moment. An idea occurred to Pat. He was thinking how some company for the evening wouldn't be bad and she was at least an eight. He just needed an opening.

Then he remembered, "You still working that perfume counter in Sears down at the mall?"

"Yea, but they cut my hours. It was all right for a while. Brad and I were able to spend a lot more time together, the rotten louse."

"Who's that, your boyfriend?" Pat was real curious now.

"Was! With all the time I spent with him he still found time for that bitch, Cathy. Caught them red handed. Oh, they tried to cover it up." She paused catching her breath. "To hell with both of them." She looked sharply the other way and obviously was still upset over the breakup.

Pat saw his opening and made his move. "Hey, I'm sorry things got so messed up for you. Sounds like you got a raw deal. Some guys are like that I know, gives the rest of us a bad name. Not all guys are like that you know. Look, I was just getting a few things and going home to watch the game on TV. If you want you could come over and watch the game or just hang. I don't mind the company and it looks like you could use some."

Her first reaction was to turn down the offer. She was uptight and still smarting over the breakup. She really didn't need any complications right now, but after taking a minute to think about it she realized that she really could use the company. It might be better then sitting home sulking all evening, and going with her girlfriends from work to a bar just to meet a stranger wasn't too appealing either. Sheryl and Rhonda tried all afternoon to get her to join them tonight at Evie's Place for a drink and some dancing. She was a baseball fan, even played on a girl's softball team not too long ago, and Pat at least was honest about his way with women. No ties or strings attached here.

She looked at Pat and said, "Yea, not such a bad idea, even if you are a clumsy oaf." She laughed as she looked at the two clerks picking up the cereal boxes. Pat had to laugh at himself. She pulled her cart away from the mess and turned it down the next aisle over, "Let me finish here and I'll head over to your place. You still in that apartment over on Hampton?"

"Yea, number 47, bottom floor on the corner. Just park on the street in front. There's usually plenty of room. See ya there." She nodded and Pat headed for the beer aisle actually more excited than he expected which kind of surprised him. What surprised him even more was the way Sue came over to his apartment and made him dinner while they watched the game. She only cooked up some burgers on the Hibachi but whatever she put into them was fantastic. They had burgers, chips, and beer while they watched the Giants win a close one. Not only was the game exciting but Pat found Sue was too. When they finished dinner and the game she gave him the best dessert he'd had in a long time.

Chapter 4

Maria comes into the bedroom after checking on the kids. She doesn't exactly tuck them in, they each believe they're a little too old for that anymore, but she does make sure they're settled in for the night. They're finally asleep. It took a little longer than usual since today they each had a traumatic experience of one sort or another. She did notice however a change in the kids after Antonio got home and talked to each of them. Theresa was in a much happier mood and seemed to have forgotten her earlier problem with whatever happened to her at school. She was pleasant and bubbly at the dinner table, which was more like her usual self. She even said she wanted to wear her new dress back to school on Friday.

Maria was pleased her daughter liked the dress. She had been afraid Theresa wouldn't like it, and her efforts at being what she considered a real mom who made her kids clothes and lunches would fail. Maria believed a real mom made clothes for her kids and canned her own vegetables and made jams and preserves at home. She remembered how she went to school more days than not wearing clothes her mother had made her. They simply couldn't afford store bought clothes and home made was a necessity. Kids today don't have a clue how easy they have it and what their parents went through. Maria wondered if all parents think the same way in each generation.

Even Ryan was cordial and polite through dinner and beyond although it did seemed a bit forced. Maria didn't know what Antonio said to him but it appeared to be working. Ryan knew of course. He knew he was going to behave himself no matter what it took. There's no way he was going to let his sister take his fishing trip away from him. Antonio always had a way with the kids. She wished he would spend more time with them and get more into their lives with the things they do at school and at home.

Still, he was a better father than most and she figured she should be grateful for that, though she remembered how her father was always there for her and her brothers. Those were fond memories and she wanted her children to have the same. She knew her dad would have made a fabulous grandfather had he lived.

Cigarettes and cancer were the killers. He was a heavy smoker and enjoyed what he considered his only vice and felt he was entitled to it. He smoked over two packs a day and wouldn't slow down even after the first signs of the disease began tearing him up.

The kids never really got to know their grandfather, as they were quite young when he died. Theresa only has vague memories of him and Ryan none at all, as he was only about six months old at the time grandpa passed away. Maria is happy that neither she nor Antonio smoked. Maybe they would still be around when their grandchildren were born. Perish the thought she said to herself. I'm too young for that yet.

As Maria heads into the bathroom to brush her teeth and prepare for bed, she remembers bedtime when she was a little girl. Her dad would tease them and pretend to be brushing his teeth while he made sure they were brushing theirs correctly. He would stand behind them and make funny faces in the mirror and weird gurgling noises. Afterward he would chase them all to bed and frequently read them a bedtime story.

She knew Antonio loved her and the kids but he wasn't the bedtime story reading type and that task fell to her when Theresa and Ryan came along. She didn't mind, but neither did she have the knack for reading and telling stories like her dad. He could make the funny sounds and silly voices to help make the stories come alive. When she tried to do the same for her children it just didn't seem work. Theresa and Ryan were pleased with her efforts but then they had nothing else to compare them with. Maria felt it was a shame but sometimes you just have to take life as it comes and make the best of what you have.

She finished brushing her teeth and looked at herself in the mirror. Though time lines were just starting to show she still had her youthful good looks. She knew she was attractive and could still turn heads when she walked down the street. She could see the stares from the corner of her eyes and was flattered as long as the stares didn't become offensive. An occasional whistle or catcall from a passing car of young high school boys was not uncommon. There was a rare invitation on one or two occasions to cheat on her husband, though she would never consider such an act, it was flattering that she could still invoke that kind of response from other men.

Antonio was her life for better or for worse, in sickness and in health. They weren't just words to Maria but a life time commitment. She knew that no matter what happened she could count on the same from Antonio. They were committed to each other. That was one of the things that made all the problems worth while. It was something that some of her friends couldn't count on. It was getting late and time for daydreaming was over.

Antonio is already lying in bed with his eyes staring at the ceiling but off into his own thoughts. He was thinking of where he is going with his life and the lives of his wife and children. He's in a reflective mood, which bothers him. It's been happening more often and he doesn't know why. He never really thought of himself as one who thinks too much or too heavy but he has spent a lot of time doing it lately. At first he wondered if he was going into a depression but couldn't figure out what he had to be depressed about. Things may not be the greatest but they weren't that bad either.

He looked toward the bathroom as Maria came out turning off the bathroom light and heading for bed. She climbed in beside him and snuggled up close. He put his arm around her and held her tight. She hadn't noticed his mood until she realized the lamp next to his side of the bed was still on. When he didn't turn it off right away, as was his usual habit, she asked him what was wrong. He told her about Theresa's problem at school with the dress and how her friends treated her. He too was happy to hear her say she was going to wear the dress again on Friday.

He explained how he handled Ryan's situation. They laughed over that one because they both knew Theresa wouldn't go fishing if offered as she hates fishing and thinks it's boring. She went once with her father and while she enjoyed the time spent with him, she found nothing exciting about putting a live wiggling worm on a sharp hook that could poke you and get all that slimy stuff all over your cut and give you a nasty infection. Yuck! Maria felt that should solve the problem with Ryan for two weeks, but after the fishing trip she was sure things would return to normal. Antonio would have to come up with new and imaginative solutions.

Antonio suggested he would find out more about Ryan's little league requirements and would what is expected of him as a father of a player, and keep tabs on how Theresa's friends handle her renewed attempts at wearing her homemade dress to school. Maria was upset at how Theresa's friends treated her but promised not to let on that she knew. Maria is elated to find an attempt on Antonio's part to do more with the kids. She didn't press him on it, not wanting to upset the apple cart. She didn't want to scare him off. She likes this turn of events. They talked a while longer about how they would try to be better parents and give a little more to each other. They made love and afterwards Maria lies awake in the dark with her back to her snoring husband wondering what's happening.

He never has been a deep thinker or one for discussing things on levels beyond the immediate, but this is the third time they've had similar discussions in the last several months. It was not like Antonio to talk like that. Something was going on, but she has no idea what. On one level she was happy about his attempts to bring them all closer and get involved in the kids activities. She had been hoping for that kind of participation in family togetherness for along time. It was exciting for her to believe it was finally happening, but why now? What brought on these sudden unexpected discussions of where they were going with their lives? It just wasn't like Antonio. It was totally out of character. She was worried about him but she knew she couldn't show it. She wasn't sure how she should react or how Antonio would react if she did. For now she decided to just roll with it and see where it goes from here. She liked the direction, but she hoped this was for real and not just a temporary phase.

Antonio wakes up just before the alarm goes off. He never has figured out why he wakes up then, but he knows if he doesn't set the alarm he won't wake up at all for another three or four hours. He wonders if any scientists have studied that one. You'd think that if you wake up before it goes off, what's the point of setting the alarm. He tried it once and was three hours late for work. He told Pat he just forgot to set it. He knew if he'd told the truth Pat wouldn't let him hear the end of it.

He gets up and heads for the bathroom feeling more tired than he thought he should. It was a fitful restless though dreamless night's sleep. He goes through his usual morning routine wondering why he didn't get a normal eight to five job like everybody else. He knows the answer. Married not long out of high school, a child nine months later, and few if any skills left him with limited options. When the job at the sanitation department came along he realized he wouldn't find a better paying job with fewer requirements anywhere else. It actually gave them a pretty decent standard of living compared to many of the crowd he used to hang with in high school. He really was quite lucky, a beautiful Italian wife who could cook, two fantastic kids. What more could a man ask for? He should thank the good Lord for what he has and make the most of it. There's nothing wrong in wanting more, but you need to appreciate what you have first, or getting more won't really mean anything.

Before he heads out the door for work he looks in on both kids and finds them in peaceful sleep and hopes their dreams are pleasant. He stops by the master bedroom once more and watches his wife as she lies there asleep and counts his blessings. She could have done a lot better he says to himself. She certainly deserves a lot better. He vows that he will make every effort to be a better husband and father. As he goes out the front door and heads for the bus stop, he has no idea he will never see any of them again.

Traffic is light as Pat pushes his '72 Mustang through the early morning mist on empty streets lit by flashing neon signs. The misty fog is thick and wet enough to blur the colors filtering through the moisture collecting on the windshield. He was thinking how this was going to be another one of those days where nothing goes right. It doesn't take much to start a day on a sour note and there just ain't no getting' it right again once that happens. He remembered now why the relationship with Sue, if you could call it that hadn't lasted, couldn't last, very long.

She was one of the few women Pat had ever known whose appetite for sex was greater than his own, and keeping up with her was more than he or his ego could handle. He hoped she would be gone by the time he got off work, because there was no way he could handle two nights in a row with her. In fact he needed a rest. He didn't know as he pulled into the yard that he would never have to face that problem again.

Chapter 5

Pat parked his car still trying desperately to keep Sue off his mind but finding it difficult. The more he tried to shift his train of thought away from her the more it seemed to drift right back. It was frustrating the hell out of him. He got out of the car slamming the door and went into the shack to sign in. Antonio was already there drinking a cup of hot coffee talking with Guido and a couple of the other drivers Robert Hamilton and Jim Gonzales. Antonio had a knack for getting along with just about anybody.

Even in high school he had a way of making friends even with guys who didn't get a long with each other. This ability helped Antonio act as peacemaker when individuals and even groups of kids were ready to have it out with each other. School officials recognized Antonio's ability and called on him more than once to help settle issues between students. It was a talent that came in handy hanging around with Pat too long. The Dean of Boys once tried to get Antonio to run for student office but there was no way he was going to embarrass himself that way. Maria tried to convince him to run but that was not going to happen.

Pat didn't always see eye to eye with everyone. He was one of the guys Antonio had to bail out of trouble more than once. Pat didn't always know the difference between when to speak up and when to shut up. That caused him more problems than just about anything else. Tact was just not one of his virtues. Robert Hamilton was one of those people that seemed to rub Pat the wrong way. It wasn't anything in particular that Robert ever said or did to him, they just didn't get along. Of course it didn't help that Robert was a die-hard Dodger fan having come originally from southern California. Baseball season made issues between them more intense. Most of the time they were able to keep things friendly and congenial. Most of the time.

It did help Pat knowing that the Giants won a close one last night and the Dodgers got blown away at home by the worst team in the league. He started feeling better already, the problems with Sue taking a back seat now to something much more important. He wandered over to the coffee pot and poured himself a cup. Robert knew what was coming and braced himself for it. He wished it would come from someone else instead of Pat. That would make it easier to take. Unfortunately it was getting to be a habit this season. Pat took a sip of his coffee and joined the guys at the table.

"Anyone see the game last night?" Pat asked.

"What game was that?" Antonio inquired innocently knowing what was coming.

"Hey, man. The Giants were on TV last night and won a real tight game against the Reds. Hell of a game. Too bad you missed it," Pat said to Antonio ignoring Robert just as if he wasn't there. Jim isn't much of a baseball fan or one of the brightest guys around and inadvertently draws first blood against his partner.

"Didn't the Dodgers play last night, Bob?" he asks Robert, thinking he is helping his friend but realizes his mistake when he sees the look on Robert's face.

Pat jumps right in, "Yea, but you know, I think they lost. Hey, Robert, what was the score? I didn't catch that." Antonio snickers. They all look at Robert expectantly.

He gets up in disgust grabbing his lunch bucket and heads for the door telling Pat, "As if you didn't know. Just wait. The Giants won't make it out of June playing over 500. They never do. Another June swoon." Jim followed his partner out the door hanging and shaking his head.

"Hey, man, that's just an old wives tale. The Giants will be in the playoffs while the Dodgers will be home licking their wounds wondering what happened," Pat retorted. Antonio and Guido laughed with Pat as Robert and Jim leave the shack.

Guido checks the clock on the wall makes a face and shouts at Pat and Antonio, "Stop the bullshit and let's get to work. There's garbage needs picking up."

"Oops! Guido must be getting hungry. He didn't eat breakfast so now we have to get his lunch," Pat says. Antonio cringes as he knows cracks like that upsets Guido about as much as remarks negative of the Giants would anger Pat. They put their cups down in a hurry and head for the door with Guido scowling at them from behind. Slamming the door on their way out they can't help but enjoy the moment at Guido's expense. They head for the rig putting on their gloves and climb into the cab.

Today is Pat's turn to drive the rig as they trade off the driving responsibilities each day. Neither of them really cares to drive as the constant stop and go is a royal pain in the rear, especially in this heat. One of their biggest pet peeves is drivers going through the neighborhoods in a hurry having trouble getting around the rig on narrow streets where they are working, and honking their horns cussing at them as they drive by. They'd cuss louder of course if their garbage didn't get picked up.

Agreeing to trade off the driving each day was no big deal to either of them, which made the decision an easy one. They can't run the air conditioner with the engine idling most of the time. The engine will over heat plus they spend more time walking outside than sitting inside anyway. The little time in the cool cab would be more of a tease than a real relief from the heat. Besides, only a few of the rigs were so equipped. They just happened to have one of them. Radios aren't allowed in the cabs as that slows them down according to Guido. Sometimes partners don't always agree on what station to listen to and that has caused some hard feelings, though that wouldn't be a problem for Pat and Antonio. They pretty much agree on most issues that come up between them including what kind of music to listen to.

They file out of the yard with the other rigs as they each head for their assigned routes. Pat and Antonio's Thursday route takes them to the east side of town in a sprawling section of twenty to thirty year old homes and small shopping centers and strip malls that pre-date the huge shopping malls going up on the north and west side. It is an older section of town known as the Eastridge Estates, but kept up well with a combination of older retired folks and younger families with smaller children, not many teenagers. Antonio thinks the small number of teenagers is in part why the neighborhood is still a pretty decent one.

Many of the homes are similar in design, plain ranch styles with the only real difference being the way families landscaped the yards with trees, shrubs, smaller plants, brickwork, and the like. As in most neighborhoods there are the good, the bad, and the ugly and sometimes the worse, but for the most part this area has maintained a gentle quiet charm that keeps the home values as well as the family values high.

They start their run on East 2nd Street and Maple Avenue, then work their way west and south till they finish their area, which is normal, or fill their rig first, which only happened once. That was after one Christmas when Santa must have been especially generous. Christmas wrapping paper and Christmas dinner leftovers was the bulk of the trash. The paper was blowing up and down the streets as the overflowing cans couldn't hold all the trash in the face of heavy winter winds. They didn't mind the wind as much as the wet. Winds actually made their job a little easier. After all, it wasn't their job to chase paper up and down the street. That was somebody else's problem, namely the street sweepers. But the rain would soak the trash after winds and kids took lids off the cans and the added water weight simply made the cans that much heavier to pick up.

They can't wait till the city gets the new trucks with the hydraulic lifts that pick up the cans at the curb and all they have to do is sit in the cab and relax. Summer was almost upon them, although the recent unseasonal heat wave would have you believe it has been here awhile, and the heaviest trash now would be the empty beer bottles. Made you wish everyone used beer in cans, or recycled, or both.

While the work progressed no different than any other day Antonio couldn't shake the feeling that something was amiss. Nothing he could see or hear, nothing visible that Pat or anyone else would recognize or point a finger at and say 'Hey, what's that?' Things just haven't been exactly right for a while now. It's almost as if something has been building for several months and he can't quite put a finger on it.

Things that never bothered him before sure seemed to bother him now. Watching people get upset over everyday mundane things annoyed him now where before he never gave it any thought. He even discovered that the same things he would get upset over a few months ago didn't seem as important now. The conflicting feelings and emotions have him reeling. He sometimes doesn't know if he is coming or going. He has been able to hide his inner turmoil from everyone except Maria.

Several times over the last few months he's talked with Maria about things important to both of them concerning feelings toward the children and each other, kinds of discussions they've never had before. He can't bring himself to tell her everything, or anyone else anything about it. It all seems to be part of the same atmosphere of uncertainty that has been plaguing him. Antonio doesn't know what to make of it.

He would occasionally stop and look around the neighborhood, up and down the street, almost like he was expecting to see something that might explain it all and he could end this madness with a nice 'oh, so that's what it is, OK.' But of course there wasn't anything marching down the street, or running out of a house, or falling out of the sky like Chicken Little to clarify everything once and for all. The last thought made him chuckle.

"What's so funny?" Pat inquired.

"Ah, nothing. I was just thinking about something one of the kids said last night," he lied. There was no way he could talk to Pat about this. He didn't want to be labeled ready for the funny farm. They continued on their route with the usual comments about the contents of garbage cans from certain houses. After you've emptied the cans of so many homes for so long you begin to see a pattern to what some people throw away, even as to how some people live. Sometimes it makes you laugh, sometimes it makes you cry, and sometimes it just makes you sick to your stomach. It's when they come across the latter type that they're glad most people are still in their beds asleep when they come by to pick up the trash. They only have to face the public during roughly the last half of their shift when people start getting up for the more normal eight to five working hours.

There's always the exception of course, the early risers, though not as early as they did, nobody else is stupid enough to get up that early, and the day sleepers who all seem to live on Pat and Antonio's daily routes and complain the most about the noise from the rigs.

They make their way through the neighborhoods uneventfully until they come to the Creighton house on East 15th Street.

"It's your turn, Tony," says Pat with a grin.

"Bullshit! And don't call me Tony." Antonio didn't like being called Tony. His name was Antonio. It was a good Italian name and he was proud of it. Only Maria was ever aloud to call him Tony and even she only did when she was mad at him and wanted to upset him. Pat didn't use it often and only when he was in a mood to give Antonio a rough time about something, like the Creighton house. "Let's flip for it," he said.

Pat took a quarter out of his pocket and flipped it high into the air. As he was about to catch it Antonio brushed aside his hand and said to let it hit the ground. Antonio thought Pat's winning percentage went up when he caught the coin. It did. Pat's uncle had taught him the trick when they lived in Sacramento years ago. He would catch the coin in the palm of his right hand and as he turned it over onto the back of his left hand, he could usually catch enough of a glimpse to know which side of the coin was going to be up. He would have just enough time to force the coin over to the other side before it hit the back of his left hand if it was going to come up on the wrong side. Antonio called heads just as the quarter hit the ground and started rolling toward the gutter. It hit a pebble and fell over, tails up.

Pat chuckles, “It’s fate, sorry.”

This whole business had to do with the now legendary Creighton house (at least among garbage collectors, meter readers, and mail carriers), and its infamous dog, Thor. Old man Creighton usually put the garbage cans outside the gate, but when he didn’t, they were expected to open it, go in to the side of the house, and get the cans. No one ever did that more than once. Not if they met Thor. He was the meanest, fiercest creature on God’s Earth according to the legend.

Former sanitation worker Jesse Hardin opened the gate one morning to empty the cans and heard and saw nothing. As he turned his back to the rear of the house and picked up the first can, he froze as he heard a low guttural growl coming from right behind him. He slowly turned around to see the biggest Great Dane he ever saw standing three feet away and looking ready to spring. Its teeth were bared and head was low and looking straight into Jesse’s eyes. The dog continued to growl as Jesse tried to think fast, not an easy chore for Jesse under the most normal of circumstances.

Jesse finally dropped the can and tried to run, but he had only taken one step when Thor was on him, knocking him to the ground and standing with his front paws on Jesse's chest and his drooling snout not two inches from Jesse's face. They stared at each other for about thirty seconds when Thor started licking Jesse's face. Old man Creighton finally came out and called Thor off, but blamed Jesse for provoking the dog. Though complaints have been filed by various victims of Thor's greetings, the fact that he never actually bit anyone keeps him home. But if you ever met Thor, you didn't want to meet him again. Jesse Hardin now works in the water recycling plant and has occasional nightmares about attacking Great Danes with massive tongues licking his face until he wakes up in a cold sweat.

Antonio forgot all his other concerns for now and concentrated on how he was going to get past this one if the cans weren't outside the gate, and Thor was visible inside. Antonio pulled his bucket to the side of the house; saw the closed gate, and no garbage cans. 'That figures' he thinks to himself. He looked back to the street and couldn't see Pat behind the rig, but could hear him empty the cans from the house on the other side. Antonio started to turn away but held up instead. The threatening atmosphere that the Creighton house always seemed to exude just wasn't there. He couldn't explain it, he could just feel it, or not feel it.

Pat came from around the rig and shouted from the street mockingly, "Having any problems?"

Antonio flinched. The hell with it he thought then marched to the gate and opened it quickly. He stood there looking for the dog, but nothing happened. "Let's get this over with," he said to himself quietly under his breath. He rushed over to the first can and heaved it up and over his shoulder and emptied its contents into the bucket, all the while looking out for Thor. When nothing happened he just as quickly emptied the second can into his bucket and was pleasantly surprised to find he was through here, and still no sign of the legendary beast. He couldn't believe his luck. Antonio started smiling as he hurried out the gate and closed it quickly with a flourish.

He pulled his bucket behind him as he marched down the driveway with a slightly exaggerated swagger and whistled a tune showing a total lack of concern.

"You son of a bitch," Pat shouted. "The last time I went in there that fuckin' dog had me pinned to the fence!"

"My, my, such language. Maybe it's your deodorant, or more likely your personality," said Antonio with a grin. He was really enjoying this.

Chapter 6

Despite the lightness of the moment Antonio couldn't shake the feeling that something was wrong at the Creighton house. Well, maybe not wrong, but certainly not right. The house always had such a foreboding presence. It wasn't just Thor. It was like the whole place exuded malevolence. On days when the cans were outside and no one had to tempt Thor's surliness there still seemed to be a sinister nature about the place. That feeling wasn't there this morning. It was more like a dead coldness he couldn't explain.

It was sort of like the feeling of being in a damp musty cold cellar, but that didn't explain it either because he was outside and a cellar was dark and inside. The closest he could come to it was a morgue. It felt like a morgue. Morgues felt the same to him whether he was inside or standing outside so that worked for him. Antonio really didn't know what to think. He was still confused, which made him uncomfortable, jittery.

He climbed back into the cab of the rig as they moved on down to the next block. Antonio tried his best to ignore the disquieting feelings and concentrate on the task at hand. Not that it took much concentrating to empty a garbage can, but he had to do something to get his mind on another tack. It was becoming increasingly difficult for him to do that. And he still couldn't understand why.

Though the sky was still dark the first hint of dawn breaking could be seen on the eastern horizon. The temperature was supposed to be cooler today but only marginally. You could already feel the warmth in the air. No cooling breeze coming from the bay area over the hills on the west made the warm temperatures feel even warmer. Some of the lawns in the neighborhood were beginning to brown with the combination of warm weather and water rationing that had already begun due to low rainfall this past winter and spring. A few automatic lawn sprinklers were starting to come on now. All watering had to be completed by six a.m. or you faced a stiff fine for violating water-rationing ordinances put in place to conserve the short water supply.

Antonio focused on weather and water related issues to keep his mind occupied on something tangible.

He didn't want to think about anything else. He was better able to continue like this as they worked their route for several more blocks. It was possible for him to concentrate on a single thought blocking out everything else kind of like meditating. The only problem this created was having other people think he was an unsociable clod. When he put himself in such a trance he was totally oblivious to anything or anyone else around him. Maria was used to these spells and knew it usually meant Antonio was bored with either the company they were keeping or the location they were at and this was his way of dealing with it and tuning everything out.

The sky was beginning to lighten a little as Pat was coming down a driveway across the street from Antonio. He was saying something to Antonio but had to shout it louder several times to break Antonio's self imposed spell.

Antonio woke up, "What's that? I couldn't understand you."

Pat shook his head and pointed at a house across the street and down two. "You sleep walking or what? Where's briefcase?" he asked again.

Certain houses they identified by the particular characteristics of the kind of trash in their garbage cans, the kind of car, truck, or RV in the driveway, or other peculiarities of their homes, yards, pets, or the people themselves. It was something they just did out of habit without really thinking about it. A house over on Elm Street is painted a flat black with both the garage and front doors a bright fire engine red. Another on East 4th Street has an elaborate wishing well in the middle of the front lawn with a working bucket that can be lowered with a rope. These of course are the Black house and the Well house.

Over on Poplar is an elderly lady who has been most friendly to them. On a few occasions she has been up early enough to see them when they make their run. She says good morning and offers them coffee or biscuits but they kindly refuse. They fondly refer to her as Granny. Briefcase on the other hand was something of an enigma. In this case, the gentleman of the house had a peculiar routine. The car in the driveway almost always had the engine running while he completed some task or other in the house. He would come dashing out of the house running to the car with his tie flying over his shoulder, waving his briefcase, turn to blow his wife a kiss, and hop into the warmed up car and take off like he was late for an important meeting. It was the same every

Thursday. What could be the hurry every Thursday? Did he do this on the days their route took them elsewhere? They could only speculate on the rest of the week.

Antonio looked at briefcase's house. It was quiet, no sign of life. No lights were on. On the few occasions the car was gone when they came by the lights were usually on in the house. Only once or twice was the car in the driveway and the lights out like he had a day off and the kids were out of school. But usually the house still appeared to be occupied like someone was home. Now the car was parked in the driveway, cold and lifeless as the rest of the house. Even with the car there Antonio couldn't help but feel that no one was home. It just had that feel to it. It was like when you went up to a friend's house and knocked on the door and no one answered you just knew whether somebody was home or not. That's how it felt, lifeless, cold and empty.

A chill went up Antonio's spine and the hair on the back of his neck stiffened. The feeling that something was out of kilter just went up another notch. He slowly stepped into the street while staring at the house. By the time he was in the middle of the street he began slowly turning around to view the rest of the neighborhood. He looked up and down the street on both sides taking in every detail like never before. His heart started pacing a little faster. A light sweat was breaking on his brow. His head began pounding and he felt like his temperature was rising. His feet had stopped turning in a circle but his head was still spinning and the homes were still passing by his field of vision.

The morning sun was not up yet but produced enough light to give a good picture of the street without diminishing the view of lights coming from inside the homes. Except there were no lights coming from inside any of the homes. None. Not one.

Pat came back to the truck with another full bucket and watched his partner for a minute wondering what he was doing and finally saw the look on Antonio's face. Pat was puzzled when he asked, "What's the matter with you?"

"Pat, look around. What do you see?" Antonio was scared shitless. It finally hit him what was wrong. His only surprise now was that he hadn't noticed it before. It seemed so obvious. Yet sometimes you can't see the forest for the trees. That was what his grandmother always used to say. He never really understood, or even thought about it, it was just an old saying he'd heard hundreds of times before, but now he understands what she meant.

Pat looked around with little concern more to please his friend than anything else. He shrugged his shoulders and told Antonio, "Nothin', so what?"

"Nothing. Exactly. No people, no cars moving, no trucks, no motorcycles, no moving vehicles of any kind." Antonio just realized something else. "No cats, no dogs, not even a bird. Pat," his voice was shaking now, "where's Ronnie?" Ronnie was the paperboy whose route crossed theirs along the block they were on. He never failed to stop and talk with them every Thursday morning. It was part of their Thursday routine. Pat took another look around. This time however he did it with a greater degree of concentration. He followed Antonio's footsteps almost exactly as he went into the middle of the street and looked around. He carefully eyed every house, every car, every tree, and every bush looking for some sign of life or movement. Finally he looked up and turned to Antonio.

"Does seem a bit quiet don't it."

"A bit quiet, Pat? Tell me, exactly what do you hear?"

Pat turned around slowly listening intently trying to pick up a sound. Antonio jumped up into the cab and turned off the ignition. As the sound of the engine died down it became deafeningly silent. It was unnatural. Only the slightest breeze blew a few leaves down the street, a sound that would normally have gone unnoticed until now. Pat finally looked at Antonio and said, "I don't even hear the traffic from the interstate. Tony, what the hell is going on?"

Pat's fear now mirrored Antonio's. The interstate was less then half a mile away and you could always hear the traffic from this distance. It was sort of like breathing, you never really noticed it until something brings it to your attention like a cough or a sneeze. Well, they noticed it now because it wasn't there. The usual sound of tires on the asphalt, diesel engines accelerating, occasional horns honking, and all the traffic sounds bouncing off the sound walls, all of it was gone. It was eerie.

They had been working their shift since three a.m. The night was always quiet in the neighborhoods then, even some of the business districts were like neon ghost towns that time of the morning. But the interstate was always busy, heavy sometimes, lighter at others, but always traffic of some sort. Antonio knew that if the traffic had ceased all at once they would have noticed it right away, like someone turning off a light switch. But who turned off the traffic? For that matter the neighborhood? How far did this go, the whole town?

"Oh shit!" he thought out loud. If Antonio was scared before, that thought horrified him. What if this disappearing act was happening all over town? Pat tried to come up with a logical explanation for what was happening.

"Look, Antonio, maybe there's a reason for all this. You know, maybe there was an accident on the interstate, something serious, something big time, and the cops have it blocked off in both directions. It doesn't happen all that often, but ya know, it happens man. Just hope it wasn't someone we know, right?" There was an edge of panic to his voice like even he didn't believe what he was saying; trying to come up with a reasonable explanation to what seemed to be unreasonable.

Antonio looked at him while slowly shaking his head. "How does that explain briefcase's car sitting cold in the driveway, or Ronnie not coming by, he never misses a chance to talk to us? Or old man Creighton's dog not showing up? You know, I don't think that damn dog was even there." They both looked up and down the street each lost in his own thoughts and fears not knowing what else to think or say. The world as they knew it had just taken a sudden and unexpected turn, and they felt like someone thrown into a vortex and being pulled down to an uncertain end.

Pat still found it hard to believe no one was around. He was frequently impulsive in his words and actions and generally liked taking matters in his own hand. He ran up to the porch of the nearest house and started pounding on the door. The sound echoed through the street increasing the feeling of emptiness that already pervaded the scene. No one answered. He ran next door. He pounded again, and again there was no response. After the fourth or fifth house he returned to where Antonio stood in the street. They stood there in silence for several minutes neither knowing what to say, what to make of this weird situation they couldn't fathom. Pat broke the silence still trying to find some reasonable explanation, some rational logical purpose behind their illogical situation.

"Let's run down to Parker Square. There's bound to be someone there. Maybe we'll find out what's going on." Antonio stared down the street toward the small single block shopping center known as Parker Square. He had a gut feeling they weren't going to find anyone at

Parker Square either, or anywhere else for that matter. He couldn't explain it. He didn't know why he felt that way. It was just a driving fear deep down in his soul. He had an uncomfortable feeling he was soon to discover what all his feelings of foreboding for the last several months were all about. He's not so sure he is ready for it.

"Antonio! Snap out of it! Let's go!"

Chapter 7

They jumped into their rig and Pat rammed it into gear trying to peel rubber like he was driving his Mustang, but the rig reacted the way a diesel should. He built up speed as fast as he could and headed down the street toward Parker Square. When he went through the intersection at the first corner he looked both ways out of habit but ignored the stop sign. Antonio reacted instinctively and yelled at him to watch out before he hit someone.

"Yea, like who?" responded Pat.

Antonio didn't have an answer. It was a normal reaction; you stop at a stop sign. He wondered what if they were over reacting to what may be just a neighborhood quirk or if nothing was normal anymore. If this was for real then what now constituted something normal? If that were the case, would anything ever be normal again? His mind was racing a mile a minute. He thought, 'What if I'm getting ahead of myself, after all, we really don't know what the hell is going on, if anything.' He remembered a discussion in school when he and Maria were taking a psychology class at the local junior college before they got married. The discussion revolved around what was considered normal, what would pass for normal in our society, and what wouldn't. He thought the whole exercise was pretty stupid, after all, if everybody did it, it was normal, if only a few did it, it was weird. When he said so during the discussion the professor just kind of chuckled, paused, and pointed at another student to continue the discourse. Antonio felt the professor was patronizing him and was embarrassed when some of the nerdy types just snickered at him.

Well, what would they think now he wondered? If everybody pulls a disappearing act, is that normal? If only a few remain does that constitute weird? That was the next question. If most of the town disappeared, how many were left? Would they find the others? Were there any others?

He bit his lower lip and pounded his fist against the door in frustration. What the hell was going on? It was worse than his blackest nightmare and he had a feeling it was just beginning. He watched the houses as they sped by. There was no sign of life in or around any of them. Where was everyone? Where could they have gone? And not just people, all the animals seemed to have disappeared, too. Why? For what purpose? He couldn't fathom an answer.

Antonio sees the Arco station as they pass by. There is a car next to one of the pumps with the nozzle still in the car, but no one around. He realizes they are close to the shopping center. Antonio sits up straight in the seat and turns to Pat, "There has to be somebody around in the shopping center. Maybe now we can get some answers. Hope they're not too embarrassing, you know, like the president just landed by helicopter at the mall on the other side of town, and we're the only ones who didn't know about it."

"Antonio, there ain't no way half this town would care to see that son-of-a-bitch let alone the whole town. I don't care if he is the president, there'd still be somebody around. Besides, even if everybody loved the bastard, even if he was the most popular president ever, which he is far from, there'd still be some poor slob covering the phones in most offices and businesses. Especially if they have bosses like Guido. There'd always be some people who just didn't give a shit. You would still see somebody walking around. I mean this place is like a ghost town. Look at it."

Pat was turning into the parking lot at Parker Square. The number of cars they observed may have been less than usual but not by much. That much looked fairly normal. What was unusual was the lack of anyone walking around making their morning rounds of the small businesses that made up Parker Square. While it was still too early for most the stores and shops to be open the gas station on the corner normally had several cars at the pumps with people complaining about the price of gas while they filled their tanks full.

The postal drop boxes usually had a fairly steady stream of people dropping off their mail on their way to work. The grocery store opened early and always had a few customers even this time of day, same for the dry cleaners. Now the gas station lights were on and two cars sitting at the pumps but no one could be seen inside or out. The lights were also on in the grocery store but near as they could tell no one was in there either, no cashiers at the checkout counter, no baggers stuffing groceries into paper or plastic, and the dry cleaners was dark and deserted.

Pat drove slowly down the center of the north south parking lot. Where the shops had large display windows and glass doors with easy visibility to the interior no one was visible inside. Everything seemed empty, abandoned. The dry cleaned clothes could be seen hanging in their clear plastic wraps waiting for someone to pick them up, except no one was. No one was picking up eggs for breakfast at the supermarket or dropping off mail at the mailbox. It was as dead and lifeless as the neighborhood they just came from.

"Let's go to Betsy's," Pat suggested as he accelerated. Betsy's was a small coffee shop at the north end of the shopping center where they occasionally ate a late breakfast. Their Thursday and Friday routes brought them close enough to Betsy's that they ate breakfast there three or four times a month. The first time they stopped there it was convenience. The restaurant was simply close by and really the only eatery within reasonable distance from their route to stay on schedule and still get in a decent meal. Neither of them cared for the fast food breakfast variety.

They were pleasantly surprised to find the food and service above normal and the atmosphere almost homey. There was no Betsy. Benny Moore bought the place after he retired from thirty years in the construction business, made a few renovations to suit his own taste, hired people who also filled his requirements for friendly, old fashioned service, and opened for business. He named the place Betsy's and displayed a sign with a grandmotherly image because he thought people would more likely trust an old fashioned home cooked meal from grandma than they would coming from a gruff old grandfatherly type. The place was popular from the start and did a fabulous business.

As Pat pulled up in front of Betsy's they could see the lights were on but nobody was home. They jumped out of the rig and dashed into Betsy's slamming the glass doors against the back of the booths on either side of the entrance. They stopped about five feet into the café and surveyed the sight before them. Plates of half-eaten food sat on the tables in several of the booths and at the counter. Steam was rising from something on the stove back in the kitchen area. The radio on the shelf behind the cash register was turned on but only static came through the speaker. Antonio walked to a table with a half-eaten omelet still on the plate and reached over putting his finger into a cup of coffee.

"It's cold," he said almost in a whisper.

Pat walked along the counter, "It's like whatever happened, happened all at once, but not in a hurry. I mean, there's no chairs turned over, no cups or glasses knocked over, no dishes on the floor, or newspapers scattered around." He looked up suddenly. Pat ran out the door to the newspaper racks in front of the restaurant and of the three morning dailies usually on display he found only one with today's edition. It was a local paper, The Herald. Being an old fashioned clear plastic paper dispenser Pat had no trouble opening it with one good swift kick. He grabbed one of the papers and ran back into the café spreading it open on the counter. They both scanned the front page for any clues that may have presaged their current predicament. Nothing. They found the usual stories of war in Eastern Europe and drive by shootings in the inner cities, a police call for a domestic disturbance, a convenience store hold up, another school shooting this time in Arizona, but not a hint of the weird state of affairs they now find themselves in.

"One thing's for sure," said Antonio, "the way things are going, the crime rate will be dropping."

"No one around to commit them except you and me," Pat answered. They flipped through a few more pages but both knew it was a waste of time. Pat didn't even look at the sports page for the latest story on the Giants big trade that was announced late yesterday afternoon.

"Well, it was a nice try, but now what?" asked Antonio.

Pat looked over Antonio's shoulder at the radio behind the counter. He ran around the counter almost losing his balance in his haste and grabbed the radio dial turning it hard right all the way to the end.

"Let's change the channel. I didn't like that one anyway," he said.

"Give you three to one odds they're all playing the same tune," challenged Antonio.

"You may be right, but you never know until you try," Pat responded. He slowly turned the dial back to the left stopping whenever the static seemed to have something more to offer than noise. The level of static varied as he turned the dial but beyond that, there was nothing: no music, no news, no commercials, and no talk. Nothing. Their level of fear and anxiety just went up another notch. Till now all their troubles seemed to be local. Stations on the radio came from all over the area, as far as San Francisco, Sacramento, and San Jose. Pat reached the end of the dial and started back the other way.

"It's no use man, they're gone. Just like here," sighed Antonio, the fear and frustration deep in his voice. "Those stations come from all over. If this thing is that wide spread we are in deep shit. I mean, how many people are we talking about? If everybody from Sacramento to San Jose disappeared, we're talking about millions of people. Where would they go? How could that many people just up and move? It's like they were all beamed up to the Enterprise by Scotty."

"Yea, maybe, but I still can't accept the idea that we are all alone."

"Well, Pat neither can I. We must be missing a piece of the puzzle here somewhere. None of this makes any sense. We're not dreaming, we're not hallucinating, to the best of my knowledge we haven't crossed over into another plane. So where does that leave us?"

"I'm afraid to guess," said Pat. "We're not both totally insane at the same time are we?"

"It may be a crazy situation but I don't think we're both insane. You maybe, but that's nothing new."

"Up yours, Antonio"

"How do we look rationally at an irrational situation?"

Pat's face brightened, "Maybe the answer lies in looking at it irrationally."

"Oh, that's deep, especially for you. Pat, let's look at what we know," Antonio suggested.

"That ain't much."

"True, but the last time we actually saw anyone was when we left the yard. I remember a few cars on our way to the Eastridge Estates to start our route. Since then we covered about a third of the streets in the neighborhood without seeing a soul. We drove through the area to get here and still haven't seen anyone. There is nothing in this morning's paper to give us a clue, and no radio station in our listening range is on the air. What about out of state, you know, like Los Angeles?"

Pat laughed in spite of the seriousness of their plight, "Robert will love you for that."

"Somehow I don't think so," Antonio said sardonically.

Pat slapped his hand down on the counter and looked sharply at Antonio, "Parker Appliances, three doors down."

"What about them?" Antonio asked.

"They've got TVs in there. The networks can't all be out. Let's go." Pat headed for the door without waiting for a response. Antonio's level of anxiety rose again. What if this thing was more than regional, what if it was national? Antonio followed Pat to Parker Appliances though he was sure now the results on TV would be the visual equivalent of what they found on the radio.

Chapter 8

They ran down to Parker Appliances with Pat leading the way. Fear gripping each of them as they raced for the store dreading they'll find no more than they did on the radio but hoping they might find some answers. Antonio began to wonder if the answers might not be worse than the not knowing. The not knowing was driving him up the wall but suppose the truth turned out to be a worse nightmare than their imaginations could dream up.

Reaching the front door Pat nearly busted his nose on the glass as he slammed into it. He automatically assumed it would be open and was shocked when he found the door locked. They're not quite used to the emptiness surrounding them and the situations they encounter as a result of that condition. "What the hell?!" Pat slammed his fist against the glass doors.

Antonio pointed to the sign painted on the window giving the days and hours they were open. "They don't open for another hour," he said.

"Shit!" yelled Pat rubbing his nose checking to see if it was broken or bleeding. "You'd think they'd have a little more consideration for the early shoppers."

"Yea, well, nobody's shopping now. Might as well break a door or window," Antonio suggested.

"Probably set off an alarm of some sort," Pat replied as he looked around the doors and windows for any indication of an alarm system present.

Antonio thought about that. Might not be a bad idea. Just might bring them some attention though he's not so sure. "If it sets off an alarm maybe somebody will come running," he said.

"I seriously doubt it, though if they did we'd have some tough explaining to do. What do we say, we thought the town was empty so it was OK to bust the window and walk in?" replied Pat. "You know how that would sound?"

Antonio nodded as he was looking around the parking lot still hoping to see someone, anyone, come running to ask them what the hell they thought they were doing. Even a police car with red and blue lights flashing pulling up in front of the store would be a welcome sight right about now. Not like it would be the first time he'd seen police lights pull up in front of him.

When he and Pat were in high school they'd gone over to Pleasanton and trashed their archrival's school in preparation for the big game on homecoming night during their junior year. Pat turned over all the trash cans he could find that the janitors hadn't emptied while Antonio emptied a bag full of dead fish into the school's Olympic swimming pool. They had just finished spray painting 'Dublin High' on the front of the school when they saw a police car at the far end of the parking lot trying to sneak up on them unnoticed.

Pat, having anticipated the possibility of getting caught, had parked his car several blocks away and with a getaway plan that kept them close to trees and bushes most of the route back. They quickly broke for the first row of trees in the park next to the school and instantly the police lights and siren were on as the patrol car accelerated in their direction.

The row of trees ran in a line away from the street and worked to their advantage. They wore dark clothing and had purposely chosen a moonless night. Even with a spotlight from his patrol car the officer had trouble spotting them. When he finally caught them in the spotlight they had reached the end of trees at the other side of the park and dived into some bushes that ran parallel to the cross street from where the patrol car chased them. They were again out of the spotlight and by the time the officer drove his unit around the block he had lost them completely.

With some luck, a lot of patience, and a slow response from the patrolman's backup, they got back to Pat's Mustang undetected and made a clean getaway. They were school heroes for a while but word soon got around to school authorities who the culprits were. While they officially got away with it, not enough evidence to push it publicly, they were privately warned to tread lightly. They were being watched very closely. Their senior year, mostly at Maria's urging, they played it cool during homecoming week and let someone else take the risk. Someone else did and someone else got caught.

Glass shattered. Antonio turned quickly raising his arm instinctively in front of his face to ward off shards of flying glass, although most of the debris flew inside the store. Pat had picked up a large stone he worked loose from the planter box lining the front of the store and threw it into the window sending glass flying everywhere and setting off the burglar alarm. They both scanned the square for any sign of movement, that anyone was concerned about the alarm. No one was. If anyone heard it they certainly weren't showing it. It was always possible that someone was calling 911 about now but neither of them really believed they had anything to worry about, at least not on that score.

"I thought they used plate glass for these windows," stated Antonio curiously.

"They do now, but not when this place was built," answered Pat. "This shopping center is as old as the proverbial hills." He kicked the remaining large pieces of glass from the edges of the window and stepped through into the store. Antonio followed. The store was dismally dark with only minimal lighting used to help night patrols view inside the store for unwelcome intruders. New posters were on display announcing a summer sale this weekend on all specially marked TVs. Bright florescent orange tags were attached to many sets on the floor and along the wall. Antonio thought the sale would be a big flop now, after all, no people, no customers, no sales. He began to think this would make a wonderful sit-com if he weren't part of the cast.

Pat ran to the nearest TV on display and turned on the power button. Nothing happened. "Damn," he said in frustration. He looked around at the bank of TVs that lined the wall in front of him. Row after row of blank screens from ceiling to floor was staring at him. It was almost like they were mocking him, like silent sentinels in a new silent world. He wasn't thinking sit-com any more. More like weird science fiction. This was something you'd expect to see on Twilight Zone or Outer Limits.

"There must be a common switch that turns them all on at once. But where?" asked Pat.

Antonio studied the walls trying to remember the last time he was in the store how they turned on the wall of TVs. He and Maria bought a TV here a couple years ago. They arrived just as the store was opening up one Saturday morning and the sales people were still in the process of turning on all the sets for the customer's convenience. He remembered what a traumatic experience that visit was. He wanted something bigger than what they could afford and it took all Maria's strength of argument along with some added arm twisting to keep him within their budget.

Pat had just bought a big screen TV from one of the big chain stores in the mall and Antonio felt unreasonably jealous that he couldn't afford one also. Maria had to remind him that Pat was still single and didn't have the financial responsibilities of a wife and children. They ended up with one that fit their budget and their living room, that is, their parlor. It was a 32" screen with picture in picture and a fancy new style remote control that Maria gave Antonio a lot of teasing over and actually they were both quite happy with the purchase.

They started searching the wall on either side of the bank of televisions. On the far end toward the rear of the store Pat found a small metal plate on the wall and opened it. There were six small circuit breakers in two rows of three. He threw the first row of switches and half the TVs lit up. The room filled with loud static noise and light from screens covered with electronic snow. Pat and Antonio ran to them and started changing channels trying to find something more useful.

The store was on a new satellite system with hundreds of channels from all over the world. All they found was more of the same, static and snow. It varied in intensity from channel to channel, but they found no picture or sound anywhere they tuned. Antonio was reminded of the play he and Maria studied in drama class in high school, 'Stop The World, I Want To Get Off.' Now it seems like everybody has. Pat was getting more desperate with each channel change. The noise seemed to grate on their nerves in greater measure with each turn of the knob or push of the button.

"Where the hell are they? What the hell is going on?" Pat started slapping and kicking the TVs until his foot finally smashed a screen on the bottom row creating a loud pop and sending sparks and glass flying in all directions. Suddenly the lights from a hundred screens went out and the noise stopped into a deafening silence. Pat looked up to see Antonio standing at the breaker box where he had just thrown off the breaker switches.

"I have to make a phone call," Antonio said in a flat even voice.

Pat stared at him with an incredulous grin and started to chuckle mirthlessly. "Who the hell is going to answer?"

"Maria."

"Sorry, man, I wasn't thinking." Pat felt embarrassed covering his face with his hands in a downward wiping motion. "There's a phone on the manager's desk. I don't think he'll be using it right away." Pat was afraid to say what he was really thinking. Antonio rushed to the phone and punched in the number with desperate hope and an anguished heart. With the end of each ring his heart sank a little deeper, and the pain grew like a balloon expanding deep in his chest. The longer he waited the tighter his fist gripped the edge of the desk and the tighter he closed his eyes until he was in excruciating pain.

Pat, trying to ease his friend's distress, took the phone from Antonio's hand and set it in the cradle and said, "She's probably out looking for help for her and the kids. She's a good mom, she'd do that. You know she won't sit there waiting for help to come to her."

Antonio looked up at Pat. He knew Pat was right and thought about what to do next. "We'll have to go look for them. We can start at the apartment and go from there."

"Yea, but not in the rig. It's too slow. Look, there are plenty of cars out in the parking lot. It hasn't been that long since I hot-wired a car. Let's grab one and head over to your place and see if we can find them, OK?"

Antonio glanced out the window and said quietly, "Yea, let's go." Neither one of them really knew if they would find Maria and the kids but Antonio couldn't accept the idea that they might disappear out of his life just like that either. He began to wonder if the apprehension he has experienced over the last several months, all the discussions of where he was going with his life, the feelings that something was in the air, something that wasn't quite right, weren't a precursor to this event. He still couldn't figure out what this event really was, or what it means, or where this whole thing will lead them. It's like they are in the hands of some power or force way beyond anything they have any control over. He even wonders if Maria had any inkling of what was happening to him. She must have noticed something in the discussions they had, but he really wasn't sure. Fact is he isn't sure of anything right now.

Pat had already exited the building through the hole in the window. Antonio hurried to catch up. In the parking lot Pat was looking for a car he felt he could easily hot wire. Antonio started looking for a car with keys in the ignition. They both found what they were looking for. Antonio shouted across the parking lot, "I found one," about the same time Pat was diving under the dashboard of an old Chevy. Antonio jumped behind the wheel of a Ford Bronco and turned the key in the ignition. When the Bronco's engine roared to life shattering the pervasive silence Pat pulled up from under the dash too fast banging his head against the steering wheel.

"Ouch!" Pat looked up to see Antonio hit the breaks and skid to a stop next to the Chevy Pat was all too eager to test his hot wiring skills on. He was a little disappointed he couldn't continue but didn't have time to dwell on it. More important things were at hand. He hopped out of the old car and into the Bronco as Antonio laid rubber across the asphalt onto Parker Avenue heading south toward the apartment complex.

Chapter 9

It didn't make sense, any of it Antonio thought. He kept asking himself the same questions over and over. What the hell is going on? Where is everybody? Where did they all go? Why weren't the two of them in on it? Was this some sort of cosmic hide and seek? If so, then who is 'it'? He had the oddest sensation that he should know at least some of the answers. He doesn't know why he feels that way but he does. He can't think of a single solid reason why he should feel like that. Some how though it did seem to be climatic to the feelings he'd been having for the last several months.

He didn't know how to explain it. It was all so strange. It was like he knew something was going to happen, not a premonition exactly, after all, he didn't envision this, but like the air itself was charged with some psychic revelation he just didn't have the power or skill to interpret. He felt that if he had just begun to understand what was happening to him during that time he might have gotten some handle on what was going on now. Maybe. It's all so confusing and way over his head.

Oh, hell, how could anybody figure this out? I'm just a garbage collector for Christ's sake, I'm no important scientist, or psychic scholar, or famous holy man of some sort he thought. He wondered if anyone else had the same feelings of foreboding that he's had the last several months. He's still not absolutely sure that they're related, but can't shake the feeling they are. They must be. He didn't know what else to believe.

And if anybody else did have these kinds of feelings, or whatever you call them, would they also still be around? If so, where? Would they be close enough that they could make some sort of contact? Oh, my God what a mess. Thinking about it was driving him nuts. Antonio knew he must concentrate on something else. He had to get home. That was all that mattered right now. They could deal with the rest after he found Maria and the kids, if they found them. What if they didn't, couldn't? He didn't want to think about that possibility.

But Antonio was already having some trouble thinking of the apartment as home. He couldn't help but feel he was going to find no more there than they'd found anywhere else this morning. He didn't know what he would find at the apartment, but he feared the worst. Why should he expect to find anything different there? Of course they would search the neighborhood, the school, the park where Maria sometimes took the kids after school, even though it was too early for them to be there. They had to look. What else could they do?

And now a new thought crossed his mind. Was it possible that whatever was happening was a good thing? They automatically assumed that whatever was happening was a bad thing, that everything happening had a negative impact on them. Could they be wrong? Could it be possible that whatever was going on actually had a positive side, or some beneficial purpose unknown to them? He couldn't think of any. Fact is that would make less sense than any other scenario he'd come up with, but was it possible? He didn't know. Who could possibly know least of all them? After all, who the hell were they? What was so different about them that they would be the only two left out of the whole city, or county, or state? Good lord, let's not go any further.

Antonio's mind reeled. "What the hell am I thinking?" he wondered. He knew he must be going crazy. This whole business was crazy. His life and his marriage were not what he expected them to be, but oh how much simpler things seemed just twenty-four hours ago. Whatever problems he and Maria had were put into a much different perspective when compared to this present situation. He still wasn't sure what this present situation was. Or will be. Just thinking about it was making him question his sanity.

He wondered if you were still able to question your sanity did that mean you were OK? Maybe he should have paid more attention in psychology class after all. Maybe there was something in those nerdy books that could've helped him decipher this mess. Most of the work he turned in for that class Maria actually did for him. Course he did most of her math homework. The trouble for each was when finals came along neither was quite up for the exams in those classes. That's in part why they ended up dropping out. He wondered if the nerdy creeps in the psychology class who snickered at him then had disappeared also. That would be all right with him. That would mean he had the last laugh after all. Somehow though he didn't feel like laughing. So who was better off? That really depended on where everybody went, or were taken. Taken? Oh shit. That's a nasty thought. Taken by whom, or what, and how?

This kind of thinking was getting him nowhere. Antonio decided to think less and observe more. He doesn't know what difference that will make but if it will stop him from thinking too much about their current plight all the better. He started paying a little more attention to what surrounded them on the way to his apartment. He studied the buildings, the trees, the bushes, the alley ways, the store windows, the homes, especially the ones with opened garage doors, he was surprised at how many there were, anywhere that one might reasonably expect to see some form of human, or animal life. Nothing. Nothing moved. Nothing could be seen, nothing was heard. It was the same everywhere they looked.

He even looked in the sky and wondered if the planes disappeared in the air, or waited till they landed on the ground for the people to get off before they disappeared? And what about the ships at sea, or people in hospitals on the operating table, did the doctors get to sew them up before they all went poof? There I go again he admonished himself, thinking too much. He decided he was getting nowhere again. He had to stop going there. Keep your eyes on the road he reminded himself.

The streets looked like the image of Dublin as a ghost town, which is pretty much what it had become. The only difference is they would welcome a few ghosts at this point. Even ghosts would be better company than nothing, provided of course they were more like Casper than the poltergeist type. There were no moving cars, or other moving vehicles of any kind on the streets; no buses, no delivery vans, no taxis, no motorcycles, no bicycles, no emergency vehicles, no skate boarders, no roller skaters, not a pedestrian in sight, not a dog, not a cat, not a bird in the sky.

He was even convinced that if he looked through the grass in the park, or lawns of local inhabitants, or in the ground anywhere, he'd be hard pressed to find an ant, a worm, a cricket, or any other bugger. Maybe that was carrying things a bit too far, but why not? All other living things seemed to have disappeared. But why? That still remained the big question. They had no answer. That brought up the other big question. Would they ever find an answer? Or would they want to? He thought again, maybe the answer is worse than the not knowing.

The problem wasn't only outside on the streets. As they passed homes with large front living room windows, or places of business with large open display windows they could detect no one inside, no movement of any kind, or any indication that they were not alone. Neither could speak. They were awe stricken. It was beyond their comprehension. The immense implication of what they were seeing, or not seeing, was finally beginning to sink in. They were alone. The static on the radio and the snow on the TV screens was one thing, seeing the empty vacant streets, homes, and businesses was another. The visual impact from personally seeing the nothingness around them had a much greater force on them then the vicarious nature of the audio and visual media. You had to feel it to believe it. They felt it, and they were real believers.

While they hoped to find Antonio's family back at the apartment, neither one had any real expectation of finding them now. The bleakness on the streets was overwhelming. It permeated the air until it was suffocating. A look came over Antonio's face as a new realization came over him. He slowed down a little and started looking quickly left and right, front and back to confirm his suspicion. Pat knew something was up but wasn't sure what to make of it. Antonio had a way of doing that to him.

"Wh-what is it?" the anxiety showed in his voice.

"Take a look around, on Parker, and on all the side streets. Take a close look. What do you see?"

Pat was confused. He thought that was what he had been doing. He tried looking for something new or different that came to Antonio's attention that he might have missed, but he didn't see it. Finally he said, "The same thing we've seen since three o'clock this morning, man. Nothing. Not a damned thing. What the hell are you talking about?" Antonio was scaring him. Things were bad enough, Pat didn't need anything more.

Antonio continued, "How many old sci-fi movies did you see on TV when you were a kid?"

Now Pat was really confused. Maybe Antonio was losing it after all. "Sci-fi movies? Are you kidding?"

"How many?" Antonio insisted.

"Well, plenty I guess. What's that got to do with now?" Pat wasn't sure where this line of questioning was going. He couldn't see a connection or conjure one up right away.

"What did the streets in those old movies look like?"

Pat gave in. He knew all too well that when Antonio got on a roll you just had to play it out. "Oh, I don't know. Most of them had creatures that crawled out from under the sea or flew in from outer space in flying saucers or riding on the backs of meteors like in 'The Blob'. When monsters or aliens were chasing them, cars were over turned, buildings were destroyed, and the streets were a mess. Sometimes car engines were still running and people were hanging out... of... them..." His voice slowed down as it began to sink in what Antonio was talking about.

"Exactly! Like everything happened all at once, all of a sudden. No time to prepare. Bang! Big surprise! End of the world! Except there were always a few good people left around to start things over again."

Pat knew how to play the straight man. "OK, where's the mess?"

Antonio was in his realm. "That's just it. This wasn't some sudden event. There was no monster, no alien, no big bang. This was a gradual, measured, quiet removal of every living creature, man and beast, leaving behind nothing but wind and dust. And us."

Shivers ran up and down Pat's spine. "Well, I hope 'us' ain't the only ones left behind. Besides, why us? Who the hell are we that we should be the only ones left?"

Antonio replied, "Ain't got a clue, I don't have any answers. We sure can't repopulate the world. Besides, you're not exactly my type you know."

"That's a scary thought, spending the rest of my life alone in an empty world with you. I thought eight hours a day five days a week was bad enough. And you're not even cute. This is not a deserted island with a beautiful babe."

"Nope. Just a deserted world where I'm stuck with an ugly Irishman," said Antonio.

"City, deserted city, let's not write off the world just yet. I'm not ready for it," Pat was still hoping. He tried to forget for now the static on the radio at Betsy's and the snow from the national broadcast networks on the TV's in the appliance store earlier this morning. That brought a whole new dimension to their situation he didn't want to deal with right now.

Antonio made a right turn onto Beachwood Drive and the apartment complex came into view. He slowed down and they scanned the street in case they could see Maria and the kids walking for help. No one was in sight. He was not surprised. He pulled the Bronco into the parking area and stopped in front of their apartment. Maria's car was still in their stall. So she hadn't driven anywhere. Maria normally walked the kids to school so the car being in the stall wasn't in itself a bad sign. They looked at each other before getting out.

"What if they're not here," Pat asked.

"Then they're not," Antonio replied and got out.

Chapter 10

They jumped out of the car and headed for the staircase. Antonio bounced up the stairs three at a time with Pat in hot pursuit. His emotions were swimming in a sea of anxiety not knowing what he would find, but afraid he already knew, afraid his worst fears were about to come true. As they approached the apartment he could see the front door was closed. His heart was racing, his stomach was churning, and his hand was shaking as he turned the knob while smashing through the door. It flung furiously against the wall the knob punching a hole in it.

He called out her name at the top of his voice and stood there in the parlor listening to the blaring silence. Antonio was frozen in space for about thirty seconds before he broke and ran from room to room shouting all the while, "Maria! Maria! Where are you, Maria?" He kept calling her name searching desperately for any sign that she or the kids were there. He realized more now then ever how much he really loved her, and how much he would miss her. That last thought froze him in his tracks. It hit him now that she might really be gone. He feared it, but he didn't want to believe it. Now it looked like he didn't have much choice. This nightmare couldn't get much worse.

He looked into Pat's questioning eyes, "I just realized, I'll never see her again will I?" He turned facing the hall down to the children's rooms. He called their name's once each. Silence was his only response. Pat didn't know what to say. He never felt that strongly about anyone in his life and though he felt for his friend, he had trouble understanding the depth of Antonio's anguish. The only time he ever knew what losing someone close to him felt like was when his family was notified of the death of his Uncle Mike during the closing months of the Vietnam War. Pat was devastated. Uncle Mike was the closest friend he had in the world, almost the only friend. He had met Antonio at school and they had hit it off pretty good but that friendship was just developing. Uncle Mike was all Pat had. But it wasn't quite the same as losing your wife and kids all at the same time. That kind of closeness being ripped away all at once had its own kind of pain.

Pat tried hard to find the words to comfort his friend but his only response, “Hey man, your guess is as good as mine about what’s going on here. Let’s not give up yet. Maybe she walked them to school.” The word school jogged Antonio’s memory and he ran into the kitchen. There was no half eaten breakfast on the table like at Betsy’s, no back packs with school books and homework ready to go, no brown bag lunches packed and ready for the kids to take to school. Both kids hated the lunch pails from the store. They both thought they were too big to use them anyway. Brown bags made them feel older, more mature. Although on occasion Maria did let them buy a lunch in the cafeteria, she felt she could make a healthier lunch than they would get there. Lunch purchased in the school cafeteria was only an occasional treat given as a reward for doing something good.

He ran down the hall first to Theresa’s room. Her clothes for school still lay on the chair where she put them last night. Her bed was unmade and rumpled from a night’s sleep. He found the same in Ryan’s room though the clothes were not laid out quite as neat. This much was clear, they hadn’t even gotten ready for school yet nor had any breakfast.

He ran to the master bedroom and saw the unmade bed. Antonio checked the bathroom and found Maria's toothbrush was dry. It hadn't been used this morning. When Maria woke up in the morning she always brushed her teeth before she did anything else. She hated morning breath, wouldn't even give him a good morning kiss until she brushed her teeth. That bothered him most on mornings they could sleep in. She still had to get up and brush her teeth before she would climb back in bed and give him a good morning kiss, or anything else. Mornings they didn't have to get up early were few and now he wondered if it would ever happen again.

Pat stood at the doorway, "Whatever happened came down before they were up and ready for their morning routine."

"Looks that way," Antonio answered.

"Doesn't she have a friend in the apartments someone she sees a lot, or might visit early in the morning?" Pat inquired.

"Yea, Debbi, but if she were up and around you'd know it. They're kinda loud over there. In this silence she'd sound like she was here in the room with us." Antonio didn't really care for Debbi and her husband Frank but Maria and Debbi were good friends so he put up with them for Maria's sake. It wasn't so bad when Debbi and Frank were over, but it was worse when they brought their two boys with them. They were two of the most undisciplined rude kids he'd ever seen. He couldn't remember a time when they came over that they didn't break something of Ryan's, or at the very least, make such a mess that he had to help Ryan clean his room after they left. It wasn't quite fair to make Ryan clean it by himself. It wasn't his fault for the mess. Maria liked Debbi and felt sorry for her as they didn't have many friends. Antonio could understand why.

"I don't think they made it out of here this morning before whatever it is happened, but I need to look around the apartments and head for the school just in case," Antonio said quietly.

"I understand. Let's go, maybe we'll get a break finally, huh?" said Pat sympathetically.

"Thanks, that's not a bad thought," said Antonio though he didn't believe they would. They left the apartment and looked around the complex even entering several other apartments. They found a few with partially made breakfasts on the table or stove. In one apartment Pat turned off a burner with a pan ready to catch on fire if left there much longer. He had to use a dishtowel to keep from burning his hand on the plastic handle that was half melted. That brought a new fear. Gas or electricity left on in the right, or wrong places and major fires could erupt all over town. Antonio remembered the steam rising from something on the stove in the kitchen at Betsy's earlier that morning. He wondered if they should go back and turn off the stove.

"We can't waste time turning off all the burners in every house and restaurant in town. It's bound to happen and we can't worry about that now. Fact is if a major blaze did erupt, it might draw anyone still around right to it. We might find that we're not alone after all," Pat said with pleasant anticipation.

"You may be right, but I wouldn't count on it," Antonio said pessimistically. "Look, we can't do anymore here. Let's go down to the school." They got in the car and headed for Murray Elementary School. Ryan was in fourth grade and Theresa was in sixth. Antonio liked Theresa's teacher Mrs. Fernandez. She always worked with the kids like it was all she lived for, struggling with those who had difficulty and praising those who could do more with less effort, never making anyone feel uncomfortable.

Ryan's teacher, however, Antonio had hit heads with several times. In plain language the guy was a jerk. He reminded Antonio of those nerdy types in college that he couldn't stand; smart, smug, and always thought they were better than you were. He tried to get Ryan moved to another teacher but the administration said there wasn't enough room in the other fifth grade class so Ryan was stuck with Mr. Richards for the duration.

He turned onto Davona and floored it. The street was straight enough that you could see anyone walking on the sidewalk without having to slow down. They saw no one. He turned into the small front parking lot at the school and braked hard to a stop in front of the office. They jumped out Pat running to the school office while Antonio ran to Theresa's classroom. Both doors were locked. Antonio went down the hall to Ryan's classroom and it too was locked. On his way back to the front of the building he did notice a door open at the end of another hallway. He stopped in his tracks.

"Pat, down here," he shouted. Pat came running after Antonio and they found the open door that led to the janitor's supply closet. The janitor's cart of brooms and cleaning materials was in the doorway. "Did he get here to start work this morning or was this left from last night?" Pat asked.

"Now that you mention it, it could be either. The janitor is usually the last one to leave and the first to arrive. They don't sleep. It's part of their job description," Antonio said.

"Well, that's a big help. Now what," asked Pat?

Antonio was at a loss. In the new vernacular, this was the mother of all frustrations.

"Isn't there a park somewhere near here?" Pat asked.

"Yea, but they normally go there in the afternoon on warm days after school, not on the way to school," Antonio replied.

"Would they stop at somebody's house on the way, you know, pick somebody up to walk to school with?" Pat suggested.

"They might, but they would normally stay outside on the porch or at the sidewalk. We would have seen them on the way over here. Besides, you saw the apartment. I don't really think they ever left for school," sighed Antonio.

Pat thought a minute and said, "It might be worth checking out the park anyway. It's a logical meeting place for people lost and wanting to find others. It's a place to start."

"Why not? At the moment I can't think of anything better." Antonio was resigned for the moment to not having found his family. He wasn't ready to call them lost. He just couldn't give up no matter what the evidence to the contrary. He knew they had to keep on the move or go bananas thinking about it. There had to be an answer somewhere. They just hadn't figured out where that was yet. They drove through the quiet empty neighborhood several blocks south where a local park with picnic tables and a small playground sat just as empty and quiet. Antonio parked at the curb next to the playground. They sat in the Bronco scanning the park looking again for something alive and breathing but saw nothing.

"Not much point in getting out," thought Pat out loud.

Antonio remembered the last time he brought the kids to the park. Maria hadn't been feeling well so he brought the kids here to give her a chance to rest for while. Theresa found several of her friends at the playground and stayed there to play with them. Ryan brought his plastic baseball bat and a couple of whiffle balls so they found a clear spot to play a little baseball for a couple of hours. It was a nice day and he enjoyed himself more than he expected to, finding the time spent with Ryan a real pleasure for them both. He wishes now they had done it more often.

He looked around the park and noticed the building on their right. Antonio pointed to the public restrooms, "Think anybody's hiding in there?"

"That's getting desperate," suggested Pat, "If it's even open there'd probably be nothing more than a passed out drunk or green haired druggie lying on the floor."

"That's getting pessimistic," responded Antonio.

"Let's get the hell out of here," said Pat.

"Sure. Any suggestion where?" Antonio asked. Neither of them really knew what or where to go from here. Antonio scanned the houses around the park. He never really noticed it before but they were an odd combination of fifteen to twenty year old homes on three sides with some new housing lining the street on the west side of the park. The styles were quite different and he found it curious that he never noticed it before. He wondered if the values of the old ones went up with the addition of the new homes or did the old houses keep the value of the new ones down. While he and Maria were trying to save for a home of their own he also found it curious why he was thinking of home values at a time like this. I guess it really doesn't matter any more he thought. There aren't too many buyers around right now.

Chapter 11

"Let's go back to the yard. Maybe some of the other drivers have come in already. Maybe they're seeing the same things we are."

"You mean not seeing, right?" answered Antonio. "You expect other drivers haven't disappeared like everybody else?"

Pat just shrugged his shoulders. They weren't sure what to expect. Nothing they have seen in the last hour or more was what they expected. It was important to find out if they were the only ones left, or did some of the other drivers find themselves in the same position they were in, wandering around in the dark. Pat could just imagine Robert Hamilton's reaction to this sort of situation. He'd go nuts, completely out of his gourd thought Pat. Picturing Hamilton that way gave Pat a kind of sadistic pleasure. The thought of that Dodger lover freaking out made him smile. The fact that they were in the same dilemma kept the smile short lived. Maybe we're lucky and Hamilton was among the missing thought

Pat. The thought caused him a small pang of guilt but that was short lived also.

Antonio was thinking how Guido was handling this strange event. If other drivers were coming back to the yard reporting people missing, that nobody else seemed to be around, Guido would simply assume the drivers were loco and had lost it. He believes most the drivers are crazy anyway so that wouldn't be too difficult. The drivers would get frustrated trying to convince him, and Guido, who had trouble accepting anything out of the ordinary, would berate them for leaving their routes and order them to return back to work, threatening them with suspension if they didn't go immediately.

That being the case Antonio thought, the more drivers present supporting the same story the easier it would be to convince Guido that something weird was going on in this town, if not the state, or even the country. Could it even be the world? The results from their search for news on the radio and TV stations was still giving him a scare to think everything could be gone, that this could be a universal event. Something was definitely wrong, but what?

On the way to the yard they had to pass through the Covington Subdivision. It was a newer housing development on the west side of town near the freeway. It was less than ten years old and quite popular with the young upwardly mobile yuppie set. The yards were small, houses big, and prices even bigger. Teenagers from other areas in town generally referred to the development as Snob Hill. Thursday was their trash pickup day and as Antonio drove through the streets of the Covington neighborhood he wondered what their garbage looked like. Probably a lot of empty caviar and latte containers and champagne bottles he imagined, no frozen TV dinners here. Then he saw a garbage rig in the middle of Malcolm Drive.

Antonio came to an abrupt stop, "Look," pointing to the rig, "whose run is this?"

Pat thought a minute, "I'm not sure but I think Snob Hill is Jeff and Todd's territory."

Jeff Anderson was a twelve-year veteran who was showing the ropes to the new rookie Todd Wallace. Todd has only been on the job about six months. At first he had more trouble adjusting to the odd hours than most new hires but had finally gotten used to it and was becoming an old hand under Jeff's tutelage. Todd and Jeff got along well and the veteran driver even has Todd interested in his hobby of model railroading. They've made the rounds of local hobby stores looking for the right trains for Todd to start his layout and convinced his wife to park her car in the driveway so he can begin building the table for it in the garage. When driving partners have common interests it makes the working relationship run smoother. Most of the driving crews share a common interest.

Todd is a newly wed and that was cause for some humor at his expense concerning why he had difficulty adjusting to the early hours required for this job. He handled it well and that helped him get accepted as one of the guys. If you were too thin-skinned you didn't last long around this crew. There were no women among the drivers but they all knew that would just be a matter of time. Their only concern was what type of personality the first woman would have and how would she adjust to their sense of humor and ribald teasing.

"Some 'butch dyke lesbo women's libber' is all we need," as Pat put it was their greatest fear, not that any of them really knew what that meant. They wanted someone who could fit in as one of the boys, but still be a woman. Until a woman actually joined one of the crews it really didn't matter. They mostly stayed away from the topic and would just wait until it happened and deal with it then. Guido figured no woman was dumb enough to want to work with these guys in the first place.

They drove slowly around the rig scanning the driveways, trees, and behind cars looking for any sign of the missing drivers. Antonio stopped the car jumped out and headed for the rig. The engine was still running so he jumped in the cab and turned it off putting the keys in his pocket. He rounded the back of the rig and found the crusher was in an up position awaiting more trash to compress into the hull. One of the buckets was in the rig apparently having just been emptied, but where was the rig's crew Jeff and Todd? Antonio walked toward the sidewalk when Pat called out.

"Hey Antonio. Look here," Pat said with his hands out to his side in a gesture of asking what gives. He was standing by the other bucket sitting on the sidewalk full of garbage. There was no sign of Jeff or Todd. The streets here were as empty and silent as anywhere else they have been all morning. No lights on in any of the houses, no one running to the car late for work, no kids heading out on their way to school. There were a few sprinklers going connected to automatic systems watering nearly green lawns.

"Want to bang on any more doors?" offered Pat.

"Hell no. That's your department." Antonio visually inspected the neighborhood noting the continuing silence with combined disgust and fear. "Besides, I doubt anyone would answer, but then you were probably used to nobody answering your knock even before all this nonsense," he said with a grin.

"Up yours," responded Pat with his usual platitude. "Let's get back to the yard. Maybe we'll find some answers there." Pat didn't sound too convincing. Antonio's frustration at this point was wanting desperately to find answers so he could locate Maria and the kids. The not knowing was killing him more than anything else. Of course he wanted to find them alive and well, but if the only choice was dead, or never knowing at all, he preferred the closure of placing them in some final resting-place. He didn't think he could live with never knowing.

They continued on their way to the sanitation yard hoping to find other rigs and drivers trying to answer the same questions they have been asking now for a couple of hours with no success. As they approached the yard they saw no dust kicked up from the tires of rigs moving about the dirt parking area, first bad sign. Getting closer they could see none of the day's rigs were back from their appointed routes, second bad sign. Entering the gate and heading for the shack all seemed unusually quiet, for a normal day at least, third bad sign.

"I don't like the looks of this," sighed Antonio quietly as he parked the car in front of the shack.

"Let's ask Guido if he knows what the hell is going on," said Pat.

"You really think he's here?" replied Antonio astonished at Pat's suggestion. "You gotta be kidding."

Pat kept his mouth shut as he climbed up the steps and entered the shack, Antonio following close behind. The shack was empty and warm. The overhead fan above Guido's high-backed chair was off. Even this early on a hot day the fan was normally on, as Guido couldn't handle the heat any more than a penguin in the desert. In another hour the shack would be boiling like an oven.

"Guido hasn't been in the shack for at least an hour." Pat stated the obvious.

"Yea, but just look around. See if you can find anything," advised Antonio. He began looking through papers on Guido's desk. A large chore considering Guido's filing and eating habits. Pat checked the book to see if anyone had signed out early, no one had. A full shift had signed in and as far as the company was concerned everyone was still out on their routes putting in a full days work. They may be in for a big surprise come the end of shift. Assuming there was anyone left to be surprised.

"If we don't sign out by two are we on overtime?" asked Pat. Antonio smirked. "After all," continued Pat, "we haven't finished our route yet, and at this rate we won't be done by two, don'tcha know." He wore a big smile with the last remark. Antonio had stopped listening to his partner's relatively poor attempt at humor and was pulling up a note from Guido's desk.

"Do you realize that at the moment we could walk into any bank or place of business and simply walk out with all the money and nothing or no one would stop us? But what good would it do? We can also take anything we want and don't need the money in the first place. Here, look at this. What do you make of it?" he asked Pat handing him the note. Pat took a close look trying to read Guido's well-known poor quality penmanship. Anyone else would have been recommended for medical school based on the scribble Guido called handwriting, but no one knowing him would ever make that mistake in judgment, Guido in a white frock with a stethoscope around his neck? It wouldn't be funny at all.

"Hard to decipher this shit he passes for writing, but, I think it's something about Hamilton calling in wanting to know, what? I can't read the rest of it," said Pat.

"I could be wrong, but it looks like he wants to know 'where is Jim'. The rest at the bottom is some kind of remark concerning Hamilton's sanity. The kind that Guido gives all of us." Antonio took the note and went back to the desk.

"You think that Dodger lover is still out there?" quizzed Pat.

"Don't know for sure but there is another note written on his desk calendar says 'now where is Hamilton'. But it's written on the 4th and today is the 18th if I remember correctly," said Antonio. "The writing looks new to me and the same ink as on the post-it note here."

"Sounds like he tried to call Hamilton back and got no answer," Pat conjectured.

"Your guess is as good as mine, but I think you're right," agreed Antonio. "But what in the hell does it all mean? I don't get it, I just don't get it."

"You want to go look for Hamilton? After all if there is a chance of finding someone else out there, even if it's that jerk Richard, we need to know," insisted Pat.

"I think it's a waste of time. Where's his route today, do you know," asked Antonio.

Pat went to the schedule board, "It should be on here. Let's see Thursday, Hamilton, east side over near Wells Middle School."

"We can't just go chasing empty rigs. You know we'll only find what we found on Snob Hill," retorted Antonio. "It's too bad Guido didn't write the times on those notes. It would have been interesting to know when that all happened."

"There's nothing more we can do here. Let's go," said Pat heading for the door. Antonio followed thinking there must be something more here but not having a clue as to what that might be, he couldn't argue the point. They got in the car and Antonio put the key in the ignition but didn't turn it. He had not a clue where he was going.

Chapter 12

The day was turning into a real scorcher. The early breeze from over the hills died down and removed the only cooling agent for the area. One of Dublin's bragging points over the rest of the valley has always been the cooling breeze that came over the hills from the bay area during the summer months. Dublin was almost always a few degrees cooler than Pleasanton, and especially Livermore, which was father east in the valley and usually the warmest. On the infrequent occasion the breeze left during the day it always returned by late afternoon or early evening. The air conditioner would be back on. The physical discomfort created by the heat added to their emotional stress and compounded the situation.

Pat broke the silence between them, "The only bigger place I can think of where people might go to gather and look for other people might be the sports grounds over by the freeway. It might be worth checking out."

"Think we'll find any more people there than we have anywhere else?" Antonio replied cynically.

"Hey, man. Snap out of it. The best way to find out what happened to your family now will be to find out what happened to everybody else. We can't just willy-nilly run around everywhere without some idea of what we're doing. We may not know exactly what we're looking for but it's got to be something out of the ordinary, ya know."

Antonio sighed and looked at his friend, "Yea, you're right, you're right. I know you're right. It's just that the old saying about not knowing what you have until you lose it has hit home. I think the worst part is the not knowing. They gotta be somewhere, all of them. People don't just disappear in mass like they all fell off the edge of the earth."

"Sorry, Antonio, but if we're going to be any help to them we have to get moving." Pat pointed at the keys in the ignition, "Let's head over to the sports grounds. We can decide what to do after that on the way there." They realize now that they need a course of action. An organized search plan would allow them to concentrate on the job at hand while keeping their minds off the unreal situation they find themselves in. Antonio heads for the sports grounds via Amador Valley Boulevard crossing Parker Boulevard and starts making a right turn only to slam on the breaks in the middle of the intersection.

He points north toward Parker Square, “Look.”

Pat lowers his head a little to look out the driver’s window and sees the large black billowing cloud of smoke rising from the general direction of the shopping center. He knew it was bound to happen but seeing it begin made his stomach turn and his heart sink.

“So it starts,” was all he could say.

“Must be Betsy’s. It won’t take long for the whole strip to go up,” Antonio said sadly.

“Want to check it out for onlookers? Might be the best chance yet to find out if anyone is still around besides us,” Pat suggested.

“Right,” Antonio agreed. He spun the steering wheel around and floored the accelerator peeling rubber through the intersection. They were going seventy down Parker Boulevard by the time they got to the Square. Betsy’s was fully engulfed, as was the beauty shop next to it. The insurance office was well on its way and the fire had a start on the appliance store. Fire alarms were blaring but you could barely hear them for the noise from the blaze itself. They never realized how loud a fire sounded. They had to shout to be heard even from the street and inside the truck.

Antonio drove slowly by the center as they watched the fire destroy not only part of their town, but part of their lives as well. Home wasn't just their respective apartments, but the city of Dublin itself. They were raised here, Antonio from birth, and Pat since fifth grade, the homes they lived in, the schools they attended, the stores they shopped. It pained them to see the destruction and know they were helpless to do anything about it.

"Lord help us," said Antonio.

"Are you kidding? He's probably the one responsible for all this," replied Pat.

"What's that supposed to mean?"

Pat looked at Antonio, "Hey, maybe this is judgment day."

"What are you trying to say, that Armageddon was quiet?" asked Antonio.

Pat looked at him, "Arm a what?"

"You know, like in the bible, Armageddon, the end of days, the final battle between good and evil, God and Satan. Except it was supposed to be the biggest nastiest battle of all time or something like that."

"What the hell do you know about the bible?" Pat never heard Antonio talk about the bible before or any other religious stuff. He was just joking but this talk about the end of day's business was scaring him even more. He knew something weird was definitely going on here but he some how assumed they would figure it all out, and sooner or later things would sort themselves back into order. Some sort of normalcy would eventually return. The thought that things could never return to normal, that this was it, was more than his mind could handle at the moment. Antonio was saying something to him.

"What?" Pat inquired.

"I said I went to Catholic school till the sixth grade. We had this one nun, Sister Ann Marie, who loved to drill Revelations into our heads when she thought the class was out of order. Tried to scare us with it, make us behave. It scared a few but bored most of us. Never thought much about it till now," Antonio reflected.

They reached the end of the shopping center and Antonio stopped in the middle of the street next to Betsy's. The sound of the burning conflagration was almost deafening and the stench of burning wood, plastic, fiberglass insulation, filled the air making it hard to breathe.

They looked around in all directions in faint hope of finding someone running to see what was happening at the shopping center. Fires and explosions were always big draws for the gaukers, rubberneckers, and curious thrill seekers and it seemed odd that such an event would lack an audience of some kind. There was no audience. No one came looking.

"If this doesn't bring anyone here I'd say the likelihood of anybody being at the sports grounds is pretty small," said Pat.

"You're probably right, but the civic center and the police station are right next to the sports grounds. We should check them out," responded Antonio. "Maybe they took some calls early on when this whole business got started."

"Could be, but I doubt it," said Pat.

"Why not? Somebody might have noticed something funny and made a 911 call. There's always some nosy busybody calling the cops for every little thing. We could go in the police station and find the 911 tapes and play some of them back," suggested Antonio.

“You been watching too many of them ‘COPS’ shows, man,” Pat laughed and shook his head.

Antonio was getting more frustrated, “I can’t believe nobody saw or heard something.”

“Why should they? We didn’t,” Pat reminded him.

“Somebody must’ve had a feeling about this thing besides me!” Antonio said more to himself then to Pat.

Pat turned his head sharply at Antonio, “What the fuck are you talking about? What feeling? What do you mean besides you? Do you know something I don’t?”

Antonio was sorry he let it slip out but he was in it now. He knew he would have to come clean with Pat and tell him everything. While he feared being made fun of before things started happening he knew things were different now. In a way he was glad to get it out.

“The last several months I’ve had these weird, I don’t know, feelings,” Antonio began. “That’s the only way I know how to describe them. It was like something was out of kilter, or out of whack, things just weren’t right. There wasn’t anything I could point to, or put a finger on. Things that never bothered me before seemed to bother the hell out of me all of a sudden, and things that did bother me before just didn’t seem to matter anymore.

I was confused and anxious, I didn't always know whether I was coming or going. I have not a clue what it was all about. I was constantly expecting something to happen and it just seemed like nothing did, till now. I don't even know if it has anything to do with what's happening now, but I can't get it out of my head that they are somehow related."

Pat shook his head, "God Antonio, why didn't you say something to me? I know there were times lately you seemed distracted, but I figured there was something personal between you and Maria. I thought if you wanted me to know about it you'd tell me when you were ready."

"And what would you do? I come up to you and say 'Hey Pat, I'm feeling weird today' and how would you have reacted, huh? I did talk to Maria some but I couldn't explain it to her the way I felt it. We talked about us and the kids, but to tell you the truth there were days I thought I might be going through some kind of depression. I didn't know what to think."

"We've been friends a long time, man. I think you could've come to me and let me know this was serious. It bothers me that you didn't come to me with it." Pat tried to look his friend in the eye but Antonio turned his head away embarrassed. “Is there any more? You’re not holding anything back on me are you?”

Antonio finally looked his partner in the eye and said, “No Pat. That’s pretty much it. Actually it seems almost trite talking about it now, but while it was happening to me I thought I was going nuts. You’re right, maybe I should have trusted you more with it, but I didn’t really know what it was or what I could have told you. I still don’t know what it is.”

“Well, that much goes for both of us. Look man, no more secrets. That goes for both of us, OK?”

“Right. Keeping secrets now would be kind of difficult anyway. Let’s get the hell out of here.” Antonio pulled a U-turn and headed back towards the sports grounds. As they passed the side streets each checked out their side of the vehicle for any sign of life. There was still nothing. The emptiness remained. At this point Antonio ignored stop signs, red lights, and speed limits. No point in worrying about that stuff now. As they passed the last major intersection before the sports grounds they saw another column of smoke off to their right.

“One of the restaurants over by Gemco probably,” guest Pat.

“Won’t be the last I’m afraid,” Antonio sighed.

Antonio was thinking if this continues the whole town could end up in ashes and they might have trouble finding a place to stay, or food to eat, or even take in a movie. That brought another thought to mind. If everybody is gone and all the towns’ burn up, what do they do, where do they go? And for that matter, what would the point be of going on anyway? What kind of life would they have left? This line of thinking wasn’t helping. He needed to get back on track.

“When we get to the park where do we start?” he asked Pat.

“Assuming we don’t see anyone in the park, and I can’t believe we will at this point, I guess we follow up on your earlier suggestion and check out the police station. I don’t think we’ll find any 911 tapes. I think those calls go to some other central location for the county, probably one of the sheriff’s stations somewhere.”

“I think you’re right,” said Antonio as he made the last left heading down Dublin Boulevard for the sports grounds and the civic center. As they approached the park on the right they saw another small shopping center across the street almost fully engulfed in flames with alarms blaring. This time he didn't even slow down except to turn into the driveway that ran between the ball fields and the civic center buildings. No one could be seen on the open grass ball fields all the way to the small playground at the other end of the park. This was where the local Little League played most of their games. Ryan wanted to start this season and Antonio knew he couldn't put it off any longer. All his friends played and Ryan just wanted to be one of the guys. While Antonio had pretty much decided it was time he gets more involved with his kids he now wondered if he would get the chance.

Antonio headed for the back of the civic center building where the entrance was actually located. He stopped in front and parked in the red zone absolutely fearless of getting a ticket even with dozens of police cars in full view. It was as quiet here as anywhere else. No tickets were being issued today.

Chapter 13

Except for the lack of people running from office to conference room, to copier machine, to water cooler, the civic center building looked no different than usual. The building was shining in the morning sun with sunlight reflecting brightly off the tinted pane glass windows. The lawns were freshly mown and neatly trimmed and the floral landscaping adding bright color to the pleasant scene. Everything appeared normal, sort of.

As they walked through the main entrance they still couldn't get used to the eerie quiet emptiness that surrounded them now wherever they went. It was actually worse here because the high ceilings and lots of open space gave the interior of the building a cavernous appearance. Their voices echoed off they walls. They could almost expect to see bats flying around and hanging from the ceiling, if there are any bats left.

Neither of them had ever been inside the building before so they both stood there in the foyer taking in the view. The civic center complex was a comparatively new structure when compared to the county government buildings that Antonio was more familiar with. His contact with them was limited to getting his marriage license, paying parking tickets, and serving on jury duty for the Superior Court of Alameda County both at the Oakland court house and the newer one in Hayward.

He was elated about the trip into Oakland with Maria to get their marriage license but he absolutely hated the ride during commute hours when he had jury duty. He was inclined to vote the defendants guilty no matter what the evidence in the case just for putting him through the morning and afternoon commutes to and from Oakland. He even mentioned that to an attorney during jury questioning and was kicked off the jury with an admonition from the judge about his civic duty and responsibility. While the older county buildings put him off the new civic center they entered here impressed him.

"So this is how they spend our tax dollars," observed Antonio as his voice echoed through the room.

"Not any more it would seem. If we don't start finding people I believe those days are gone," reminded Pat.

That brought Antonio back to the present. The building may be newer and prettier but he was sure it was just as empty as he believed the government offices in other parts of the county. From the way things were beginning to shape up it appeared every place was going to turn up empty. This was not going well. Something had to give. He just didn't know what at this point. He looked around and saw the building directory on the far wall. Tapping Pat on the shoulder and waving him over, they approached the board and started reading the directory.

"Shall we visit the office of the Mayor, the City Manager, Public Works Director, oh, how about the City Fire Marshall? It seems he's been lax in his duties so far this morning," quizzed Pat.

Antonio replied, "I think they all have."

"Hey, let's not get political my good man. Besides, did you vote for any of these characters in the last election?" Pat asked.

"I don't quite remember. You see, it all depends on what color their hair, their eyes, and what they were wearing on Election Day." Antonio tried to sound serious but it didn't work. He came across more mockingly than intended.

Pat shook his head and said, "No wonder Maria wore the pants in the family."

"Keep her out of this, and don't mention her in the past tense. I'm not ready to accept that yet," Antonio warned him though not too sharply. He still wanted to believe they would eventually figure this all out and find his wife and kids. "Pat, look here." Antonio pointed to the board where it said, Emergency Command Center - Room B-100.

Pat read, "B-100. That's probably in the basement. We need to find a way down there." They started looking for a staircase or an elevator. Antonio found the elevator doors around the corner on the left from the directory board. There were three buttons marked 1, 2, and 3, but no B for the basement.

"What's this?" Pat exclaimed.

"Maybe they figured in an emergency the elevators would be out, so you'd have to use the stairs anyway. Let's look on the other side," Antonio shouted. He ran back around to the right of the directory board making a left turn and found a door marked stairs and pulled the handle. The staircase went both up and down. Without saying a word he ran down the stairs with Pat hot on his heels. A rather plain set of double doors with small vertical wired windows was at the bottom of the staircase. They could see through the wired windows that the room inside was dark. Antonio tried to open the doors but found them locked. He pounded on and kicked the doors in frustration.

"You know what this means don't you?" Antonio asked.

"Yea," Pat replied. "They never opened the Command Center." They stood there a moment pondering their finding. Obviously whatever happened did so without enough time to allow a real emergency response from local authorities. At the same time it happened slow enough to keep people from falling over each other in crowded places and making a big mess. So far they haven't found anything in the way of ramshackled buildings, car accidents, chaos in the streets, only the start of fires from unattended heat sources. With no one around to fight the fires though that could become a real disaster in its self. What could've happened to cause this kind of scenario they couldn't fathom?

"All right, let's go upstairs and check out the police station," advised Antonio, "Though it's looking more and more like they were caught off guard as much as everyone else. Why should they be any different?"

“This keeps getting stranger by the minute,” Pat said shaking his head in consternation. “Somebody had to have seen something coming. This is impossible.”

They went back to the building directory where it showed the location for the Dublin Police Department as Building B. They figured it would be faster to go out side and around to the Police building than to waste time looking for an interior door they were sure existed connecting the two facilities without having to leave the building. They were sure our exalted city fathers wouldn’t want to get wet and cold during the rainy season as they went between buildings on the people’s business. Of course it wouldn’t be located in an obvious location for the general public’s use.

They ran around to the front to the police department entrance and busted through into another quiet empty eerie room with only the hum of computers and a noisy flickering fluorescent light directly over the receptionist’s counter. Every thirty seconds or so they could hear an electronic pinging sound coming from a computer on the desk in the far right corner. Pat walked up to the counter and stated matter-of-factly to a non-existent receptionist.

"I'll be back," reminiscent of Arnold Schwarzenegger in the movie The Terminator.

Antonio cracked up shaking his head. "You idiot," he said. "Are you going to go out and drive the truck through the front door now?"

"Only if you guarantee me that Linda Hamilton is in the back room lying on the couch," Pat insisted.

"In your dreams," laughed Antonio. He ran over to the counter hopped up and over to the other side landing a little less gracefully than intended.

Pat laughed, "Why don't you just go through the gate…oomph!" He came to an abrupt stop slamming into the small door when it wouldn't open as he tried to pass through. Antonio reached over pushing a button he could see under the counter and guessing what it was.

"Allow me to buzz you in you clumsy oaf," said Antonio shaking his head. The buzzer was loud and grating but short-lived as Pat fell through the door almost losing his balance. He ended up leaning over a desk of Detective Richard Lasco, Vice Squad. Pat started to push away when he noticed something on the detective's desk. He reached over and picked up a report sitting where someone had been looking it over before they went home last night or disappeared this morning.

"Oh, shit."

"What? You find something about this mess we're in?" Antonio inquired.

"Not our mess. You remember Steve Gibson from English class our senior year?" he asked.

"Yea, that weirdo, what'd he do?"

"His place has been under surveillance for suspicion of drug activity. Seems some of the neighbors are complaining of the high volume of traffic in and out of his place over there on Wingate Drive. Looks like an under cover guy was going in there today to try to make a buy." He looked up at Antonio. "I always thought he was a nerdy little twit."

"The cops would have been in for a little surprise," stated Antonio suggesting he knew something Pat didn't, which was true.

Pat looked at Antonio with a little side-glance, "What's going on that I don't know? That maybe I should've known. You're holding out on me. We said no more secrets, remember?"

"Steve has been running a little bookie business out of that place for almost a year now."

"How the hell do you know that? And why the hell didn't you let me in on it? You been making bets on the side?" Pat questioned him incredulously.

"Hey, one question at a time," said Antonio. "I don't make bets, you know that. But your favorite Dodger fan bet all the time. I over heard him telling Guido about it one day while I was signing in. You came in late that day and we had to hurry to get on our route and the whole thing slipped my mind. I only heard about once after that."

Pat turned around and said in utter amazement, "Well I'll be damned. I never would have dreamed it. If he's been doing this for almost a year he must have been doing pretty good. I can't believe I never heard about this."

"You almost did. Over at Ernie's. Paul was going to tell you when I over heard Ernie jumping on his case threatening his knee caps if he told you about it. Ernie was afraid you'd bet your rent money away on Giant's games."

"He's probably right. I guess I'll have to thank him next time I see him, if I ever see him again."

"Which brings us to the reason for our being here in this den of iniquity in the first place. Let's search the other desks for reports of anything more pertinent to our situation," urged Antonio.

"Yes sir, boss," retorted Pat eagerly.

They searched the desk tops finding nothing more than a few mundane reports on family squabbles and minor traffic accidents. They found the desk of the Duty Sergeant and discovered the last call-in was a report of a suspicious noise outside an apartment on the west side of Dublin, but no indication of whether the report was acted on or not.

"What ever happened didn't bring any warning and caught everybody off guard," said Antonio stating the obvious.

"This was real helpful," complained Pat as he slapped a handful of police reports back down on the Duty Sergeant's desk. "So now what?" he asked. They both stood in quiet thought for a few minutes before Antonio finally raised his head and spoke up.

"The mall is the next biggest location where we might expect to find someone. Let's go on over there," he suggested. The Stoneridge Mall was located on the other side of the freeway in Pleasanton and was a popular shopping and gathering spot as it was not just the only mall in the tri-valley area but the only shopping area of any size or consequence. Several other shopping areas are in the planning stages but nothing the size of Stoneridge. They leave the Police Station and walk out to the Bronco but before Antonio can get in Pat stops him.

"I got an idea."

Antonio follows Pat's stare to the west side of the parking lot and sees a line of police cruisers along the fence. "You've got to be kidding. You're not serious?" Antonio queries.

"Oh yes I am. Wait here." Pat runs back into the station and comes out a few minutes later waving a set of keys. He hurries over to the line of cruisers and starts looking at numbers on the vehicles until he finds the one that matches the number on his key ring. "This is it," Pat says ecstatically. He jumped in the cruiser and turned the ignition. The engine roars into life and Pat searches the dash for switches to turn on the lights and siren. Soon the eerie silence is broken with the wailing sound emitted from the cruiser. Antonio shakes his head.

Pat smiled at Antonio and said, "Now we ride in style."

Chapter 14

They turn west on Dublin Boulevard lights flashing and siren blasting heading for the mall in Pleasanton. Antonio has mixed emotions about going to the mall. He knows it's a place where they might find others who may have survived this strange phenomenon or whatever it is that's happening to them, but he also remembers the pleasant times he had there with Maria and the kids. Anytime they went shopping at the mall they made an adventure out of it, eating lunch at one of the fast foods if it was Saturday, or having dinner at one of the more elegant restaurants if it was a week night.

On one occasion they took Theresa to spend money she received for her birthday the weekend before from grandma and grandpa. Though it was a Thursday there was no school the next day due to some sort of teacher's preparation day. The money was burning a hole in Theresa's purse so they decided to make an evening of it and take the kids to the mall, let Theresa spend her money, and have a nice dinner at the new Italian Restaurant that just opened up about two months earlier.

There were two toy stores in the mall plus several game and hobby shops to choose from so it took what seemed like forever for Theresa to make up her mind, especially to Ryan. He was fit to be tied by the time she ended up buying some clothes in the latest styles to impress her friends instead of toys or games as expected. She was growing up, too fast for Antonio's sake. He and Maria got a laugh from Ryan's remark about how his sister was learning to shop just like mom.

Antonio wondered if there would ever be anymore evenings like that one. Hope may spring eternal for some but for him it felt like the spring had sprung. He didn't want to lose hope but the evidence was mounting concerning the chance of ever finding anyone else alive. Actually, they hadn't even found anyone dead either. How weird was that? That made the whole thing even stranger. It was one thing to find dead bodies all over the place, but to find no one, dead or alive, anywhere that was just weird.

There was one advantage of having no dead bodies lying around. They didn't have to worry about disease from decaying corpses, or the odor, or the flies.

The picture of Maria and the kids lying dead rotting in their apartment flashed into his vision. He knew the apartment was empty but he couldn't picture them in that condition anywhere else. He didn't want to picture them in that condition anywhere actually, but he couldn't clear the vision from his mind."

"Damn," he said in a loud anguished voice.

Pat slowed down wondering what was happening, "Antonio, you all right? What the hell is wrong?" He could see the pain in his friend's face.

"I just keep seeing Maria lying dead someplace along with Theresa and Ryan. I feel so damn helpless not knowing what's going on and what's happened to them," cried Antonio.

"Hey, we're trying to find answers the best way we can. I don't have any more clue as to what's happening than you do. We have to keep looking. For now that's all we can do."

"I know, that's what's so frustrating. There seems to be so little we can do," said Antonio as he sat up straighter in his seat and started searching the passing streets and buildings for any sign of life.

Pat sped through the intersection making a fast left turn fish tailing the vehicle as he heads up and over the freeway. He slowed down at the top of the overpass as they viewed the scene on the 580 freeway below. The freeway could be seen from the civic center but their concentration had been on the building complex and attention to the freeway was minimal. Now looking down both in the east and west directions they were amazed. Pat stopped and turned off the engine as they both got out of the car. A few cars and a number of big rigs were stopped on the road in the lanes they had been traveling. No people were in the vehicles or walking around them. No doors were open on any of them like they had stopped to get out. The whole thing was like an oversized kids play set of life sized Hot Wheels cars and Tonka trucks. What little breeze there was provided the only noise as it blew dust and leaves across the roadway. A small Confederate flag was flying from the top of an eighteen wheeler with an Alabama license plate.

A small mini van was close below them. An empty infant carrier was strapped in the middle seat near the window. In the lane next to the mini van and a little behind it was another big rig with what appeared to be a half eaten fast food breakfast sandwich on the dash and a coffee in the cup holder. Pat was straining to see inside the truck's cab. Antonio looked in the cab but couldn't figure out what Pat was looking for.

"What is it?" he asked.

"I was just trying to see if I could figure out what gear the truck was in," answered Pat.

"Of course," responded Antonio. "If everyone disappeared instantly the vehicles would all still be in gear and the now empty cars and trucks would crash out of control. But they're all stopped in place." Antonio turned and ran to the railing on the west side of the overpass and saw no vehicle off the road into a fence or crashed into one another. All the vehicles were stopped in the lanes idle and empty.

"It's the same over here all the way up the Dublin grade," Antonio stated. "That means everybody had time to slow down or stop. So did they disappear from their cars, or did they have time to get out?"

"Hey man, if they had time to get out, we have to assume something strange, or weird, or different was happening. Something was going on completely out of the ordinary. Now, if everyone was getting out of their cars to see this it would be logical to assume some of the car and trucks would still have their doors wide open. I mean, not everyone would automatically close their doors in a situation like that."

"Like what? What kind of situation Pat? And how come we didn't see it and everybody else did?" asked Antonio in frustration. "Explain that one to me will you because I haven't figured that one out yet."

"Hell if I know man, neither have I," Pat responded. "But I don't think we'll find the answer here. Let's get over to the mall."

"We won't find the answer there either and you know it."

"True, but I have an idea," answered Pat. He was formulating a plan but hadn't quite thought it all out yet. Pat realized they needed to get better organized in what they were doing and decided to look at their search like a hunting trip. He remembered the way he and Uncle Mike would spend weeks prior to a hunting trip planning when, where, and how they would go. They would plan what to take in the way of food, clothing, and camping equipment, gear they would need to get the prey and for carrying it out if their hunting was successful. He would treat their search as he would a hunting trip. The only difference was now they were hunting for living people.

They reached the mall and started from the north end outside J. C. Penny's and slowly drove around the mall on the eastern side toward Macy's on the southern end. As they passed the McDonald's Antonio remembered the time they had lunch there and Ryan dropped his ice cream sundae on his lap and got so embarrassed he wanted to go home before any of his friends who might be at the mall happened to see him. Theresa held back making any remarks and Ryan was all the more infuriated feeling she was mocking him even more by not making any wisecracks as he would have done to her.

Pat continued driving up the western side of the mall and parked at the curb next to Capwell's side entrance. While they saw a few cars scattered around the parking lot they saw no one either in the lot or through the windows in the stores or the mall entrances. The eeriness wasn't getting any easier to take just because they found more of it. Everything appeared closed up from where they were sitting.

"We'll have to look for an employee entrance somewhere. The store entrances are probably all still locked," Pat suggested. They got out and looked around both sides of Capwell's entrance for a side door of some sort but with no luck.

Pat spoke up like he was thinking out loud, "I seem to remember dating a girl who worked here. Not in Capwell's I mean, but here at the mall. I remember dropping her off at work one day at a special door but I can't recall where that was."

"You've dated all the single girls for miles around and some of the married ones," Antonio retorted. "It's amazing you're still alive."

With that remark they looked at each other. Pat said, "Right now I think I'd agree with you. I'm just not sure if that's good or bad."

"Do you remember where this girl worked?" asked Antonio.

"Naw, I can't. It was too long ago." He hesitated, his face brightened. "Wait a minute. Follow me." Pat ran south down toward an outcropping in the building about a hundred fifty feet from where they were standing. He stopped just the other side of it and shouted, "Yes!" Antonio caught up with him and looked at the door half hidden in the wall. It was a special employee entrance located to keep the general public away. Pat went over and turned the knob. It opened. He looked back at Antonio, “Let’s go,” and waved him in.

They went down a short flight of stairs and into an office area full of cubicles and desks. They found a door at the other end of the room and entered a stockroom. Of course it was full of clothes but lacking in stockroom or shipping clerks. From there and through another door they found themselves on the first floor shopping area of Capwell’s. Only minimal lighting was on and the low lighting made for a surrealistic picture under current circumstances. Neither of them had spoken since entering the building. They stepped out into the aisle and each surveyed the floor.

“Now what?” asked Antonio?

“Let’s go out into the mall and see what we can find.” Pat headed for the mall entrance with Antonio following close behind. The large doors were closed so they split to each side of the doors looking for a switch. Pat found it and pushed the green up button and the gate like doors started rising. The noise seemed louder than usual as it echoed through the hollow empty mall. They walked out into the open center of the mall and scanned the lower and upper reaches of the long chamber-like hallways in each direction. It was as quiet and empty as anywhere else they'd been today, just bigger. There were no cashiers, counter people, security guards, or shoppers.

Even the early morning mall walkers were missing. These were the older folks who used the malls as a gathering place to meet and exercise by walking circles from one end of the malls interior hallway to the other. Lately they've been joined by younger mothers pushing strollers with one or two little ones in them and sometimes another three to six year old walking along side. The malls have become quite popular for this purpose for their uniform temperature control, relative safety, and convenience to shopping. In some malls the groups are large enough that they have formed walking clubs with regular meetings, special T-shirts, and planned social activities.

Now the mall stands silent and deserted. Antonio sits down on one of the malls ceramic covered benches. His worst fears continue to be realized. Pat walks over to him.

"All right, we need to make some decisions now. This thing is obviously happening all over the place. We need to decide where to go, how to get there, and what to do when we arrive. I think it's important to find out if anyone else is left wandering around like us and how can we contact them. Are you with me on that?" Pat asks.

"Yea, but where the hell do we go? Where's the best place to go? How do we find out if and where anyone else is?"

"My guess would be a large population center like San Francisco where there would be enough people to leave a few behind. After all, the tri-valley is a lot smaller area and we got left here," Pat suggested.

"No, no. Look, we need to go somewhere where someone is in charge, where some government authority has some control over the situation. Why don't we head up to Sacramento?" proposed Antonio.

"What control? You saw the civic center and the police station. What did we find there? Nothing, they were caught off guard just like everybody else. What makes you think it's any different in Sacramento?"

"Because that's where the government center is for the whole state. People would naturally expect some leadership control to come from there. Even if they were caught off guard like here, I still think any survivors would logically gravitate to that area more than San Francisco. That's where the authority is and where all directives on what to do would come from," Antonio insisted.

"Tony, there are more people in the Bay Area. I think they would naturally go to the City. It's the largest and most centrally located spot for this area," he argued.

"But all the civil government and emergency control centers are in Sacramento. All the City's ever had are weirdoes, fags, and freaks." Antonio thought a minute. "I'm going to the capitol. You head for the City if you want."

Pat tossed his head in frustration. "Antonio, we can't split up. We have to stay together. What if we really are the only two left? Look, we have to compromise somehow."

Antonio thought about that a minute. "You're right. OK," Antonio agreed. "But how do we do this?"

Pat thought a minute. It was time to put his plan into action. "Either way we're going to need supplies and a game plan. The cop car was fun but we'll need something more useful. The Bronco was good but a Suburban would be even better."

"There's several car dealerships on both sides of the freeway with plenty of vehicles with keys fresh for the taking. And the best part, no damn used car salesmen."

"There's a sporting goods store over by Gemco. We can get camping supplies, guns and ammo…"

"Guns," Antonio interrupted. "What the hell do we need guns for?"

Chapter 15

Human survival or survival of the fittest were terms or concepts Antonio had heard most of his life but had never really given much thought to. These are phrases he always put in the context of prehistoric times, or maybe pioneering days of the old west, but never something that could be applied to current everyday America. How could you? After all, wasn't this the richest, wealthiest country in the whole world? Didn't we have everything anybody could ever want or need? Why would we need to hunt and scratch for anything like peasants in some third world country?

Antonio didn't know what to think, he was shocked. The thought of needing weapons for any purpose under their present circumstances hadn't occurred to him. He never owned a gun and didn't know how to use one. When they first met in high school Pat went on hunting trips every season with various relatives, mostly cousins, after Uncle Mike died. Pat tried on occasion to talk Antonio into going along and even offered to lone him a gun. Uncle Mike had left Pat a small collection of hunting rifles. Even in high school Antonio knew that Maria was more than just a little fearful of guns and he always bowed out of any outing with Pat that involved guns. Fishing and hiking and camping out of hunting season were not a problem for anyone, so Pat respected Maria's feelings and never asked Antonio to go on any trip that might include hunting of any kind. Pat had even suggested archery hunting but Antonio knew he couldn't even deal with that. Maria would be equally upset as a bow and arrow still constituted a weapon.

"Antonio. We don't know what we're going to find out there. Yea, we haven't found any trouble yet, but that doesn't mean we won't. We have to protect ourselves against any problem we might face. And if we don't find any, we may still need to eventually hunt for our own food. The stuff in the stores will soon rot, or burn. We could be alone for a long time. Who knows how this will all sort out?"

"Well, that last part may be true. But tell me, when was the last time you saw any animal worth hunting for food around here? Or for that matter any animal worth hunting period?"

Pat looked down as he ran his fingers through his hair. He knew Antonio was right. That could present a problem later. It depended entirely on what they found in the mean time. The prospect of going on a hunting trip of any kind without his guns didn't feel right. And this was a hunting trip. Make no mistake about that. They could run into a protection problem of some sort anywhere they went. There were too many unknowns out there. He would insist on carrying weapons.

"OK, I grant you hunting may be a problem we will have to deal with later, but we may need weapons if we come up against some unknown danger. I'd rather have them and not need them then the other way around. I think they could be necessary," Pat was adamant.

"Alright, you may be right on that one. I hope not, but I can see your point." Antonio did find the prospect of carrying a weapon somewhat exciting as well as kind of scary. He secretly wanted to go on those hunting trips with Pat and his cousins but knew it would upset Maria, and he never wanted to risk hurting her feelings so he never let on his secret desire. Now the chance of actually carrying a gun brought several questions to mind. He never learned to use one but he didn't want to look stupid in front of his friend. He knew this wasn't the time to be concerned about petty feelings but it none-the less bothered him.

What if they did get into a tight situation where the guns would be needed? How much help would he really be? Would he even be a greater liability than an asset? He knew it was necessary for him to be up front with Pat. Their lives may depend on it.

“Look Pat. I never really learned how to use a gun. You’re gonna have to give me a crash course,” he said.

“That’s not a problem. We can take a few shoots in the parking lot at the sporting goods store. I don’t think anyone will complain.”

“The parking lot, right.” Antonio thought about their conversation. A few days ago such a conversation would sound like total lunacy. Taking shots in the parking lot? Now, under current circumstances, it was no big deal. Pat was right about one thing, no one was going to complain. Truth is he wished somebody would.

“Let’s get a new wardrobe. We’ll need practical clothes, jeans, lightweight shirts or T-shirts, boots or hiking shoes. We’ll get what else we’ll need from the sporting goods store,” instructed Pat. He was now taking charge, as this was more his area of expertise. Antonio wasn't complaining. They found most of what they were looking for at Miller Stockman's and headed for the exit.

"We should've brought a shopping cart," said Antonio.

"We only need a couple of each item. We don't want to be overloaded with stuff that's not necessary," Pat replied. They threw their shoplifted items into the back of the patrol car and got in.

Pat said, "Hope you paid for this stuff or I may have to arrest you."

"You'd love that wouldn't you?" answered Antonio. "You're the only one whose been arrested around here. Remember the time you were drunk at Tina's party and got into a fight with that guy after making a pass at his girlfriend?"

"Hey! She made the pass at me and I didn't know she had a jealous boyfriend standing across the room watching us," said Pat defensively. "All charges were dropped several days later."

They headed back the way they came over the freeway into Dublin to the Ford dealership. Pat suggested and Antonio agreed on a Ford Explorer for their trip. The dealer had a few to choose from and currently financing wasn't going to be a problem. It didn't take long to find one to suit their purpose with all the extra amenities anyone could ask for, and without Maria along color wasn't an issue, they picked a dark blue one. Soon they were on their way to the Gemco shopping plaza and the sporting goods store.

The store on the north end of the plaza was closed but breaking and entering was becoming an acquired habit. Once inside the store Pat wasted no time going after what they needed. Heading for an aisle on the left side of the store Pat pointed to the camping gear.

"Pick out a sleeping bag, a flashlight, some water proof matches, and some water purification tablets," Pat ordered.

"We really gonna need those? Why not just get some water bottles at the grocery store on our way out?" Antonio inquired.

"Bottles are fine for now. The tablets may come in handy later. If we don't take some with us now we may not find any later when we need them," Pat replied.

That made some kind of sense so Antonio shrugged his shoulders and grabbed the items requested. Pat grabbed his own choices and a few other things as well that he thought they might need. It was a little different from a hunting trip to get a deer but actually not by much. You still needed the same basic items for human daily existence. The differences came from the unique purpose of each activity. Problem now was no one had ever encountered the purpose of this activity before, so it would be easy to leave out something that could prove to be useful later. Now it was Pat's turn to go crazy thinking about it.

They loaded their gear into the Explorer and went back for more. This time Pat went to the gun rack behind the counter. The cases were locked but it didn't take long to find the key hanging on a nail under the counter top. That's real secure thought Pat. He unlocked the case and opened it. He looked at the rifles many of which he always wanted but could never afford. Now that he could have his pick he realizes these may not be the best for their current needs. Antonio saw Pat's hesitation at selecting their weapons.

"What's the matter?" he asked Pat.

"Some of these would be great hunting deer or bear. I've wanted that one for years." Pat pointed at a Weatherby on the end. "But any situation we encounter where we may need a gun, it might make more sense to have handguns, like these in here." He pointed to several rows of handguns in the glass case they were leaning on.

He tried another key on the key ring and opened the glass counter case. Reaching in Pat removed several guns, two pistols and a revolver, and put them on the counter.

"Now we could each use a holster," he said. Looking around Pat noticed a number of holsters hanging from a rack at the end of the counter.

"Let's see if any of these will work." They started looking through the holsters on the rack Pat grabbing one that seemed to suit him.

"That looks weird," commented Antonio. "I thought it was supposed to go around your waist."

"It's a shoulder holster. More comfortable and practical if you need to reach for your gun quickly while sitting in the car," Pat replied.

"I still can't get used to the idea that we'll need them at all," said Antonio.

"We probably won't, but I'd rather be prepared just in case," said Pat emphatically. He also wanted to reconcile the remaining difference between them. "Look man, we need to decide when we leave here, where exactly are we going? We still haven't settled that you know," reminded Pat.

"I've been thinking about that. I still think Sacramento makes more sense. But San Francisco is closer. So, why don't we head over the Dublin grade and to the west end of Castro Valley, you know, up on the hill there by the three crosses. You know where I'm talking about?" asked Antonio.

"Yea, where that big church is on the hill going over toward San Leandro."

"Right," answered Antonio, "That's the one. You have one hell of a view of the whole bay area from there. I'm willing to bet we'll see mostly fire and smoke covering large areas by then. And the freeways will be a lot more clogged with cars and trucks from the earlier commute traffic, I don't care what time this 'thing' happened, lots of people leave early to avoid the rush. We'll still see lots of cars blocking the roads."

"We can still find our way through all that," said Pat though with less enthusiasm than earlier.

"Look, Pat, you only have several options for getting into the city, all bridges which are probably clogged unless we go south and then up the peninsula. At least if the freeways are crowded with empty vehicles entering Sacramento we'll have a lot more options for getting around to the capitol."

Pat didn't want to waste time arguing. He was anxious to get going. At least they would start out the direction he wanted to go. He didn't believe things would be as bad as Antonio thought but there was always the possibility he could be right. Pat decided to go along with the plan.

"All right, we have a plan. Now let's give you a crash course in gun safety and marksmanship." Pat headed for the parking lot with Antonio following excitedly. Pat showed Antonio how to load a clip, use the safety on the pistol, and properly hold the weapon.

"Don't pull the trigger so much as squeeze it, like this," and Pat fired of a round and the windshield of a Toyota Celica about a hundred feet away cracked and showed a hole where the bullet went through. Antonio instinctively looked around as if someone might cry out in alarm. No one did. It quickly became as quiet as it was a moment ago before Pat had fired the gun.

"You try it now. Let's see if you can hit the driver side window," Pat suggested. Antonio was nervous and excited at the same time. He raised his pistol gripping it with both hands. He always wondered what it would feel like. Now he was finding out.

"That should be easy," he said with false confidence. Antonio pulled the trigger and the recoil was more than he expected. His hands went up quickly and the bullet went over the car and ricocheted of the tarmac fifty feet beyond the car.

"What the hell happened?" he said in shock.

"It's like I said. You have to squeeze the trigger, not pull it. Be aware of the recoil and keep your eye on the target," Pat said. "Try again."

Antonio was determined to hit the target this time. He concentrated a little harder on holding the gun steady and taking careful aim. He was a little more prepared for what was going to happen when he squeezed the trigger. The pistol cracked and the window shattered. Antonio shouted with glee like a little kid. Pat laughed.

"Take a few more shots and we better be on our way," Pat said. Antonio fired a few more rounds hitting windows in several cars near the Toyota. He then turned his attention to a large picture window in the front of a Mexican restaurant on the east side of the parking lot. The bullet put a hole in the window and he was a little disappointed that the glass didn't shatter as he hoped. He was ready for anything now.

Chapter 16

Each morning we wake up and think we know what the day will bring. We get up and go through our usual morning routine sometimes like a robot or in a trance until we have our morning coffee and begin to face the day with some semblance of normal anticipation. We go to work and listen to the boss, or some disgruntled co-worker complain about the job or the working conditions for the hundredth time this week. We worry or fret about meeting the deadline on our current project. We worry about the school board meeting or the candidates in the upcoming election and why we can't seem to get better qualified candidates to run for public office.

But we never seem to take the time to determine what it all really means, how any of it affects our lives or the quality of our everyday existence. It usually takes an extraordinary event, usually an unhappy one to wake us up, shake us out of our tedious doldrums to make us take a look at ourselves and where we are going. Even now, Pat and Antonio still put a greater emphasis on the small things to get through this ordeal they find themselves in. In time that will change.

They gather food supplies from the Lucky's Grocery Store and head for the freeway and up the Dublin grade toward Castro Valley. The freeway through the hills is little different than what they've already seen. Cars, trucks, and buses are stopped dead in their tracks all along the road in all lanes and on the parallel side roads that can be seen from some parts of the freeway. At several locations they did see a vehicle off to the side of the road but can't be sure if the number is more than what one would normally expect to see as neither of them regularly commutes the freeways. Those cars were just as empty as the rest.

The side roads lead to the few homes and businesses in this more rural area between valleys of populated cities. Even here they can see a sporadic column of flame from behind a grove of trees or the other side of a small knoll or hill. Pat has an uneasy feeling that Antonio could be right, that the bay area side of the hills will produce a vision of smoke and flames not seen since the great devastating fires in the east bay hills above Oakland a couple years ago. Over a thousand homes were destroyed in that firestorm. Pat sees a problem up ahead and slows down.

Antonio quickly looks at Pat and then forward. “What’s going on?” he asks. They can see the number of vehicles thicken and clog the lanes rather abruptly.

“Could be there was an accident up ahead,” Pat suggests. They both stretch their necks to get a better look but can’t see what is causing the back up. Pat cuts over to the center divider to the emergency lane and passes the line of parked vehicles stalled in the lanes. They travel about a mile around several curves when they see the lights from two CHP cruisers, a fire truck, and an ambulance flashing slowly up ahead. A tow truck appears to have just arrived on the scene. At least four cars show varying degrees of damage from a serious accident that must have happened hours earlier. One car in particular had been the center of attention as paramedic paraphernalia sits on the ground next to it. No one is around to use the equipment. It’s as if they arrived at the scene and decided to take a break and walk off somewhere leaving the injured to look after themselves.

Antonio shudders, “Oh my God. Pat, there’s someone in the car.” They both look in shock and disbelief as they can see the arm and shoulder of the driver inside the crushed green Saturn. Blood that had been flowing down the arm hours earlier was now dried. They ran to the car kicking rescue and medical gear out of their way as they went. Antonio touched the pale cold skin of the woman behind the wheel and removed his hand quickly.

"She's dead. I'd say she's been dead for some time." The woman was dressed in a pale blue business suit and looked to be in her late thirties or early forties. The odor was already less than pleasant in the mid-morning heat. Her hair was a light shade of red a little longer than shoulder length. She was a fairly attractive woman as best they could tell under current conditions.

"That's odd," noticed Pat.

"What's odd?" inquired Antonio.

"There's no air bag. Her air bag didn't inflate," said Pat.

"Maybe she had it turned off. Some people did that stupid as it sounds," remarked Antonio.

The woman's name was Becky Sorenson and she did have the air bags turned off. About two years ago her husband and daughter were in a traffic accident hit head on by a drunk driver. Her husband was seriously injured and remains on disability while her two-year-old daughter who was in the front passenger seat in a child's safety chair was killed by the inflating air bag. Becky insisted on having all the air bags disengaged on both cars she has owned since then.

"That may be, but why is she still here?" asked Pat.

"Of course! She was dead before everybody disappeared. That's the only logical explanation. If she were still alive when it happened she would have disappeared too," Antonio answered. "That means the mortuaries and morgues would still have dead bodies in them."

"Well the next mortuary we pass you can go in and verify that notion. I'll wait outside if you don't mind," Pat said in disgust. Dead animals he'd shot while hunting was one thing, dead people was something else. He simply wanted to get away from here. Antonio sensed his friend's unease. He was equally uncomfortable. He couldn't help but picture Maria's face in the woman's place.

"There's nothing more we can do here anyway. Let's get on our way," he suggested.

"Don't have to tell me twice," said Pat as he quickly trotted over to the Explorer and jumped into the driver's seat. He wondered if anyone else was injured in the crash and whether they disappeared in their poor condition or did they heal before being removed. This is crazy. I gotta get out of here.

Antonio took one last glance at the accident scene. On impulse he reached for one of the E.M.T.'s medical kits and threw it in the back of the Explorer. He hopped in and looked at Pat's quizzical frown. "First aid kit. Never know when we'll need one."

The road between the crash site and the freeway into Castro Valley was less crowded and easier traveling. Once to the small unincorporated hamlet though the sight was not what Pat wanted to see. Fires were everywhere. The small town was burning out of control. Fire was raging on both sides of the freeway but was heaviest on the right where most of the businesses were located. The left side while more residential was not as bad.

Pat tried to look through the smoke and haze for the three crosses at the church on the hill separating Castro Valley from San Leandro. He could see them only occasionally when the wind swirled and temporarily cleared the smoke. That's also the first time he noticed the wind was picking up. Normally he would be delighted at the prospect of a cooling wind in this unseasonable pre-summer heat. Now it only meant that the flames would be fanned across town from one building to the next unimpeded since there was no one around to fight the conflagration that had already begun.

"You notice the wind?" remarked Pat.

Antonio quickly looked around confirming what Pat asked, "Yea. That will make things hot. If you ever had a desire to be a firefighter now's your chance to indulge."

Pat chuckled, "Maybe tomorrow. Look Antonio, from the way things are going I'd have to say you're probably right about what we'll see when we get to the top of the overpass near the three crosses. I still want to go through the motions. We can circle around the interchange there and head back the other way."

"No doubt there'll be more fire and smoke back home by now, too." Antonio sighed. All he could think about were Maria and the kids and with all this running around they were no closer to finding out what happened now than they were hours ago. Was it a good thing that they didn't find their bodies like that woman back on the freeway? Did that mean they were still alive somewhere? If so, was it possible that he and Pat might find them yet? This whole thing was so bizarre.

Pat made the turn on the interchange heading back the way they came and stopped at the top of the cloverleaf where the best view of the bay area spread before them. While there were pockets where the fires had not reached, most of the scene in front of them was covered in smoke from San Jose on the south to Richmond on the north, Oakland and San Francisco in the distant middle. Much of it was pocketed with flames and smoke. A strange distant roar or rumble could be heard coming from everywhere and yet nowhere in particular. It was the accumulated noise of all the fires burning at once. The whole picture had a surrealistic feel to it. They were too numb to speak. They watched in dumb horror as the world as they knew it was being destroyed before their very eyes. Without speaking they turned and got back into the truck and headed back toward the tri-valley.

As they drove in silence Antonio's mind went back to his wife and children. He was still trying to make sense of this whole unnatural situation. Looking back on his life he thought he had done a very good job of trying to do things right. He worked hard at a less than glamorous job, paid all his bills, married his high school sweetheart, loved her and the kids, didn't cheat too much on his taxes, even went to church on occasion, though he could've gone to confession a few more times. So what went wrong? What's going on here? Is this some sort of punishment? Did he die and go to hell?

'I wasn't that bad was I?' he thought. "All I ever wanted out of life was to be happy. Is that too much to ask?" he said aloud.

"Don't ask me," answered Pat surprised at the sudden question, "You were better off than I was. At least you had a family. I still have what I always had. Nothing."

"You had friends, Pat. Some people don't have that." Antonio was surprised by Pat's response. He never talked about how he lived or why. If you tried to discuss his lifestyle with him or why he never settled down with one woman you found out quickly you'd better change the subject if you didn't want trouble. "Were you happy, Pat? With your life I mean?"

Pat sighed and looked out the window while he thought about the answer. "No, not really."

Antonio looked at his friend. "I know you had it rough growing up, but a lot of people do. Most of them make it."

Pat looked Antonio, "Do they? I don't know. Maybe some of them do, but I believe most of them put up a front just like me. After Uncle Mike died I had no one who really cared about me. Course it might have been helpful if I cared about someone else, but I couldn't. I was just too scared to let myself feel for anyone. Those closest to me who were supposed to care didn't. I couldn't bring myself to take the chance. I was afraid of getting hurt again. I couldn't deal with that."

Antonio noticed a tear rolling down Pat's cheek. And he thought he had problems. He was hurting over the apparent loss of his wife and kids, but his friend, his best friend in the whole world, after Maria of course, was hurting for the lack of ever having someone close enough to understand what a loving relationship was all about. Pat's was the greater loss, for he may miss out on ever knowing the pleasure and wonder of a real close loving caring partnership between one human being and another, the incredible and awesome feeling of sharing offspring who will carry on after you.

Well, they used to carry on after you. That thought snapped him back to reality. Under the present circumstances Antonio isn't so sure that will happen anymore. What if they never find anyone else, even if it's not their own close family? Who's going to carry on and how? What with civilization going up in flames, how will those remaining survive? The big question now is whose left? It can't be just the two of them. That doesn't make sense in any scenario. Maybe if they were of the opposite sex like a new Adam and Eve, but Adam and Adam? How weird is that?

"We should start seeing Dublin and Pleasanton come into view pretty quick now," stated Pat matter-of-factly. They strained to catch the view as the horizon lowered into the valley they called home. It was heavy with smoke and large bright red flames could be seen from some newly fired building in Dublin near where the 580 and 680 freeways cross.

"You realize if we were to go up 580 through Walnut Creek and Concord the buildings there are more congested and near the freeway," commented Antonio.

"You think we should go through Tracy and up I-5?" questioned Pat.

"Yeah," said Antonio.

"We might have the same problem on I-5 through Stockton," reminded Pat.

"At least it would be easier to find away around if we need to," said Antonio. "There's a number of roads between I-5 and 99 we could take back and forth. And they both go through Stockton and up to Sacramento."

Pat sat up in a better mood, “Sounds like we have a plan.” That was what Pat cared about. He needed a sense of being organized. He needed to know what was happening and where they were going. Without that, he would feel lost and without hope. It was all that allowed him to hang on. It may not be the greatest of plans, but at least it was something. They didn’t know what else to do.

Chapter 17

The drive through the valley was a sad dispiriting dismal voyage like warriors of old returning home from the wars only to find their own village had been pillaged plundered and burned while they were gone. This was home. This was where they grew up. This was where they went to school, worked, lived, played, loved, cried, laughed, and in Antonio's case, was raising his family. It was slowly being devoured by a hungry inferno with a voracious appetite. The fires raged unchecked, unhindered, and unabated across rooftops, alleys, and now with the wind kicking up, across streets and roadways.

The whole world as they knew it was changing before their very eyes and there was nothing either of them could do about it. That helplessness was the most difficult aspect of this whole situation for both of them. It gave them the greatest discomfort and pain. Even if they found Maria and the kids, and any number of other folks who may have made it through this thing, whatever it was, nothing was going to be the same ever again. The places they shopped, went out to eat, went to see a movie, or went bowling; most of them were going up in flames. Other places they frequented like the library or the post office were either burning rubble or if they survived the inferno would be of little use in the future.

They could only watch in numb dismay. Both men considered what they have lost and would have been quite surprised to know how similar their thoughts ran. Both pined for love lost, Antonio's was for a wife who was friend, lover, companion, confidant, and all things that mattered most to him, while for Pat it was all those things he never found, never knew, and now seems he never will. It started to appear to each of them though neither wanted to mention it to the other quite yet, that their whole quest might actually be in vain, that there is nothing else or no one else. Pat for one didn't like the thought and wasn't going to settle for this being the end of it. He had too much of his life unfinished yet and wasn't ready to end it now. He floored the pedal and the Explorer accelerated abruptly hitting over 90 mph before he knew it.

To Antonio he turned and said, "Right, let's get on with it. This whole scene is too depressing."

"I know. Getting all bummed out isn't gonna get us anywhere. I don't know if Sacramento is where we're going to find any answers or not. Some how I doubt it, but I don't have a better idea. If you have any bright ones I'm open to 'um," voiced Antonio in complete discouragement. He welcomed Pats increase in speed. He was just as happy to pass by the area they once called home and leave the whole distressing view to get on with the task at hand. His family may still be there and he hated leaving them behind, but if leaving helps him to find them, and in the process an answer, it will be worth it.

They were flying by the familiar sights on either side of the freeway. There was the golf course on the right and the college on the left where he and Maria attended for a while before they gave it up and got married. Seeing the college brought back memories both pleasant and uncomfortable. There were fun times in various student activities like football games and dances, plays put on by the drama department and some of the classes they took together. The other times had to do with the classes where Antonio felt less than adequate, where the nerdy smart ones made him feel like a dummy in front of Maria and he just wanted to crawl into a hole and go away. Some times he just felt like getting up and punching one of them in the face and walking out. It was those times that helped him make the decision to forget college and get on with his life. While Maria enjoyed some of the classes they shared together, she never understood what good a college education was for a stay at home mom. That was all she ever wanted to be, and Antonio was all in favor of that. He was glad they quit and got married when they did. He only wished now for a chance to make what they had better. Only now he realizes he took too much for granted.

The Livermore airport was on the right but all the planes were lined up on the tarmac. No planes could be seen on the runway either ready to take off or just coming in for a landing. Seeing the airport brought back an earlier thought, did the planes in the air when this thing happened have time to land first before the people disappeared, or did they disappear in midair and the plane crashed to the ground with nobody on board? It's not like on the freeway where all the cars and trucks just sit there empty. Guess it is really hard to know unless they actually found a crashed airplane with no bodies lying around. Pat brought Antonio out of his trance.

"Looks like we'll have enough gas to get us through the Altamont but I think we'll need to stop in Tracy to fill'er up," he said.

"These things drink up the go-go juice pretty good don't they?" Antonio asked.

"We could exchange it in Tracy at one of the dealerships there for something that gets better gas mileage. Actually that's not a bad idea," Pat thought out loud. "Who knows how long the electricity will be on to power the pumps. We may need all the gas mileage we can get." The fires in Livermore appeared to be fewer and smaller. No doubt that would change as those took hold and started spreading. They sat quietly as they rode toward the Altamont Pass leaving Livermore in their wake.

As they passed by Livermore another thought occurred to Antonio. If the Livermore Radiation Laboratory and Sandia buildings go up in flames will that release any radioactive toxins in the air? The locals joked about Livermore residents glowing in the dark due to the presence of the labs in their area. But could there really be a problem he wondered. Either way, there was nothing they could do about it now. There would be time to worry about it later when and if they come back this way.

So much is unknown about their present predicament it's hard to be sure just how far ahead they can plan.

The trip eastbound through the pass was an easy go with few vehicles to block their way. The morning commute traffic on the other side of the freeway was well on its way when this thing happened and the cars and trucks clogged the lanes in the west bound direction though they were all cold silent and empty now. Not being commuters themselves they were a little hard pressed to figure out about what time this morning this all occurred.

"Seems I recall Arnold saying he over slept one morning and was shocked at how early the commute started backing up through here in the morning. He lived on the east side of Tracy somewhere and normally leaves early enough to beat the crunch." Antonio continued, "I remember him saying he left the house an hour late but arrived at work more like two hours late. Guido read him the riot act."

Pat laughed, "Guido read everybody the riot act at least once a week. He was one of those guys who ain't happy unless he has something to complain about."

"God, Pat, do you realize we're talking about people in the past tense like they're not here anymore?"

"Are they?" asked Pat. Antonio couldn't answer. "Well, if you know where they are you let me in on it and we'll head right over there straight away. I could use a change of company 'cause you're getting old and worn."

Antonio chuckled, "As you're so fond of saying, up yours."

Except for the sight of a CHP unit with flashing red and blue lights parked behind a dark red Chevy pickup truck he had pulled over only moments before the mysterious disappearing act, the rest of the trip through the Altamont was uneventful. As the valley that was home to Tracy and other cities beyond came into view they could see fires had started there also. The mall on the north west side of town was untouched but the Wal-Mart near it was fully engulfed. On the right side of the freeway there were several fires scattered about the town.

"We'll have to pull off the freeway and find a gas station still functioning where we can gas up," reminded Pat.

"Looks like an off ramp up ahead. There's a Chevron on the right and looks like a Shell station across the street from it," said Antonio.

"I almost forgot," said Pat, "we were thinking of switching cars for something with better gas mileage.

You familiar enough with Tracy to know where the dealerships are?"

"Not really. They shouldn't be too hard to find. Let's just drive around till we find one," suggested Antonio. They passed the gas stations and headed straight for downtown Tracy. They crossed a couple main intersections looking up and down the cross streets for any sign of a car dealer but didn't see anything that looked like what they wanted. Antonio remembered taking Maria and the kids to the Tracy mall once sometime back but they never went into the town. Maria had wanted to look around and see what it was like but he hadn't been feeling well that day and had no desire to drag his tired butt around town knowing she would window shop in every boutique and antique store she could find.

They occasionally took day trips to small towns around the foothills east and south of Tracy and did that sort of thing. Normally he didn't mind. They had visited little towns like Jamestown, Columbia, Coulterville, Groveland, Mariposa, and any number of similar places. Antonio knew those outings were a chance for Maria to get out and do something different breaking away from her day to day chores and responsibilities of homebound mother and housewife. They would take along a picnic basket and find a local park wherever they were to enjoy a nice family lunch together in the great outdoors.

He wasn't prepared for that kind of adventure on that day. He knew she was disappointed and so was Theresa though Ryan seemed to brighten over the fact that he wouldn't be bored to death looking at old stuff. Antonio would give anything to be able to make that outing with the family right now. As if some finger of fate was trying to torture him they passed an antique store on the right just then.

Antonio sat up quickly in his seat, "Let's turn at the next intersection. We're not getting anywhere going this way."

"Sure. Left or right?"

"Who cares," he said, "just do something different." Passing the antique store seemed to rattle Antonio unreasonably.

Pat looked at his friend, "Hey, man, let's keep a grip on it. We need to work together pal." He was getting worried about his partner. Several times now it seems Antonio was beginning to lose it. It was strange when you think about it but all through high school and some time after that whenever they got into a jam it was always Antonio who kept a level head and got them out of tight situations. He could always depend on Antonio no matter what the circumstances. He isn't so sure anymore. He's going to watch Antonio a lot closer.

Even now Pat doesn't understand the effect of losing a wife and kids can have on ones ability to cope with normal everyday stress much less the kind of situation they're going through. It's something Pat may never learn. Pat also under estimates his friend's determination to find out what happened to his family. Antonio feels totally helpless but he knows no matter what the odds or how depressing the situation may seem he can't give up. Everything that has ever meant anything to him is gone and to have any meaning or purpose left in his life no matter what the conditions he must find them. Without them his life is worthless. He knows that now. Whatever faults he or Maria have don't matter now. There are some things that are a whole lot more important.

Antonio is aware of Pat's growing concern for him and now resolves to keep his act together and work with him to achieve their goal. The only way they can hope to discover what happened to the rest of the world is to work together to search for an answer. They have a plan. It's time to do it. He looked in both directions quickly as they approached the next intersection.

"Turn right," said Antonio.

Pat abruptly turned toward the right lane a little surprised as he was preparing to turn left and wasn't expecting instructions from Antonio. He whipped a right turn a bit quickly squealing the tires and accelerating down the road. Much to their amazement the large overhead sign of a Nissan dealership loomed ahead on the left.

"Look!" shouted Antonio as he pointed to the car lot, "of course, a Nissan Pathfinder. It gets better gas mileage than this thing and still suits our purpose."

"Let's go for it," said Pat looking at his partner hoping Antonio's lively response meant he was pulling out of his earlier mood. Pat pulled into the lot a little fast and almost slammed into a new Sentra parked near the front office. No sales people came running to convince them of the smart buys there on the lot.

"That's one thing I'll miss," said Antonio.

"What's that?"

"Used car salesmen."

Pat shook his head. They hopped out of the Explorer and located where the Pathfinders were parked on the south side of the lot. While most of them were still locked two were open and had keys in them.

"Green one or blue?" asked Antonio.

"Be damned if I care. Features on both looks to be about the same. Take your pick and drive it back so we can move the gear." Pat headed where they parked the Explorer. Antonio jumped in the green Pathfinder drove it back to the entrance next to the Ford. After moving all their worldly belongings from one vehicle to the next they filled the tank from the on site gas pump Pat found near the service area and were on their way.

Chapter 18

They left Tracy with Antonio driving their new Pathfinder up I-5 towards Sacramento. As they rode past Manteca, Lathrop, and other rural areas in between they could see smoke columns rising from numerous homes and businesses. Most of the buildings in full view had logical ignition sources like stoves in restaurants and home kitchens, but several locations gave them cause to question what could've started that one. A huge carpet warehouse was fully engulfed with no visible cause or ignition source. In another case a small mom and pop grocery store was burning while nearby homes and a feed store were untouched. The conversations about how they started kept them mentally occupied and their minds off family and loved ones at least temporarily.

Cars could be seen lined on the freeway in the southbound lanes while they traveled north with comparative ease until they approached Stockton. The morning commuters heading for jobs in the Stockton area had begun clogging I-5 into that city when the event happened. While they could circumvent the vehicles they couldn't avoid the smoke. It rose from the city center and the docks along the river thick and black. The freeway ahead was choked with smoke blown across the roadway. It was obvious they would have to get off and find a detour.

Antonio worked his way to the right shoulder and watched through the smoke for the next exit. They took the Pershing off ramp and headed east through an unfamiliar neighborhood. They soon passed a neighborhood park on the left. They scanned the grounds for any signs of life but it was as empty as everywhere else they've been this morning.

Further on whole blocks on their left were up in flames making it near impossible to turn north as they wanted. This was something their morning planning hadn't accounted for and they were flying by the seat of their pants at the moment. Neither of them was familiar with Stockton other than passing through on the freeways and now finding their way around was a guessing game.

"Make a right up here and see if we can't find another way around this," suggested Pat.

"I think you're right," replied Antonio.

They took a side street south and looked for something in the way of a major thoroughfare going east-west that would allow them to circle the burning areas. They came to a stop sign at Lincoln Avenue where Antonio surveyed the blocks in each direction as far as he could see. He knew west was blocked with fire and smoke and they had to go east before they could get back on track north to get to their destination.

"What do you think," asked Pat?

"I think we're going the wrong direction and we need to find away back. I'm turning left here," said Antonio, and he did. The street was clear of smoke though the odor from the numerous fires was still quite strong. Antonio had tied a bandanna around his face to ease the effects of breathing in the smoky air. Pat said it made him look like a hood.

"If we do find people they're likely to take one look at you and start shooting first and ask questions later," Pat laughed.

"Some how I'm not worried. Actually, I wish I could be."

They went several blocks when Antonio slowed before a large older brick building with wide steps leading up to the front doors. It was the Church of the

Annunciation, the Cathedral for the Diocese of Stockton. He pulled over and stopped in front of the Cathedral. Pat looked at the building and turned back to Antonio.

"What are we stopping here for?"

"It's been along time since I last went to church, or even prayed. I think it's long over due. You can wait here if you want, but I'm going in. I won't be long. I have to do this Pat." Antonio pulled off his bandanna from his face and climbed slowly up the steps into the Cathedral. Pat considered following him in but though he was catholic, he was never brought up in the faith and wasn't very religious. He decided to wait in the car for his friend.

Antonio went through the second set of doors into the sanctuary dipped his finger into the bowl of Holy Water and crossed himself. As he glanced at the altar and tabernacle a flood of memories hit him with enough force to stop him in his tracks. All the memories of his catholic youth came before him, his first communion, confirmation, and most vividly his wedding day. He remembers how beautiful Maria looked coming down the aisle and how lucky he felt that day that this was the woman he was going to spend the rest of his life with. Now he hopes that is still possible.

He also remembers the days his children made their sacraments. They were just as beautiful as their mother was and he felt such pride in watching them. Antonio can't quite put a finger on why they stopped going to Mass on a regular basis. There wasn't one reason he could point to that put a stop to it. It just seemed to happen, or not happen. As time went by since their wedding a lot of things seemed to stop happening. What he'd give now to bring that all back for another chance. Is it really too late he wondered?

He continued on about half way up the aisle stopping at the end of a pew, genuflected, moved into the pew and knelt on the kneeler to pray. He didn't know what to say. The last prayer he remembers saying was to help Maria teach the kids how to say grace before dinner. Maria used to take care of helping them say their bedtime prayers; though he joined them on occasion it was rare. My God has it been that long he thought. He even wondered if he should be saying confession first, but to whom? Didn't seem to be any priests around. They weren't immune from the great disappearance. So why were he and Pat the only two who seem to be left?

"Why Lord? Why me? Why us? What is going on Lord? What do you want from us? You gotta give us a clue Lord, a sign of some sort so we know what we're supposed to do. We're like lost sheep. We're groping here in the dark not knowing what to do, where to go, or what to expect next. I'd like to know what has happened to Maria and Theresa and Ryan. Are they OK? Are they hurting, or in pain, or is everything all right with them wherever they are? The rest I could deal with a whole lot easier if I just knew they were OK. Yea, I know I haven't done all the right things Lord, but I have tried to be the best husband and father I could be. I know I could've done better but give me another chance and things will be different, I promise." That sounded trite. Isn't that what everybody says when they are faced with disaster or some extreme emergency? No atheists in the fox hole right?

Antonio stopped and shook his head a little and smiled, "Lord, I know how that sounds? I guess you've heard it before." Some of his early catechism was coming back. "Forgive me Lord for all my sins. I know they are many. If I tried to list them all now we'd be here all afternoon and Pat would probably leave without me if he hasn't already. Besides, you know them all anyway. We need help, Lord. Please help us. Show us what the hell we're suppose to do. Oops. Sorry Lord."

Antonio buried his head in his hands not knowing what to say or do next. He racked his brain trying to decide where to go from here. He just didn't know. "Give us a clue, Lord, something, I'm begging you. Amen." Antonio crossed himself and got up leaving the pew. He faced the tabernacle, genuflected then turned and walked out. Pat was outside the Pathfinder leaning on the bumper. He stood up as he saw Antonio coming down the steps.

"Well, that make you feel any better?" he asked.

"Yea, actually, it did," replied Antonio.

"Well, I hope he explained all this to you because anything this cataclysmic wasn't man made. It's all his fault. He's the one responsible for this. You know that, right?" Pat challenged. Pat never was a religious person and he had little to say for those who were. He put no stock in prayer, faith, or God.

"You may be right about that part, Pat, but if that's true, than there must be a good reason for it. We just haven't figured out what it is yet."

"You got to be kidding. What the hell is good about this? You've lost your whole fucking family. The whole world for all we know is gone, kaput, disappeared before our very eyes, and you think there might be something good about it? Are you out of your fucking mind?" Pat was angry. His pent up feelings were finally going to explode. Pat turned and slammed his fist on the hood of the car. It hurt but he refused to acknowledge it.

"This whole thing makes no sense at all. There's got to be other people around, we just haven't come across any of them yet. I don't know what you think is good about this but from where I stand ain't nothing good about it. You hear me? Now maybe God is punishing me for something, assuming of course there is a God, but if that's the case than he's been doing it all my life. I had parents that didn't give a shit whether I lived or died. I never got a break my whole fucking life. No one ever gave me a break. I had to do it all on my own, and what do I have to show for it? Nothing, not a damned fucking thing." Pat slumped to the sidewalk sitting with his knees to his chest, his elbows on his knees and his face in his hands crying out his pain.

Antonio went over and squatted next to him putting his hand on Pat's shoulder. He had never seen Pat express his pain over his lot in life like this before. He'd always managed to keep it inside. Now Antonio wondered if that had been such a good idea. Maybe Pat should've confided in someone to ease his pain, let it out.

If Pat had learned to deal with his pain earlier he might have found someone to share his life with instead of always being afraid to form a close relationship with anyone. Antonio wonders if he has been that good a friend after all. Maybe he should have been there to help Pat over his pain instead of allowing him to bury it all these years.

"We all get dealt a different hand Pat, some better than others. What about Uncle Mike? I thought he was a lucky break for you. Could you have made it without him? Wasn't he always there for you 'til he went to 'Nam?"

"Yea, sure. But then he got his ass blown up by a damn 'Cong booby-trap."

"But you're still alive. Is this the way he would have wanted it for you? Living from one broad to the next, never settling down to make a family of your own? You didn't have to let it be like you were growing up. You learn from their mistakes and make it better, do right what they did wrong." Antonio was at a loss for anything else to say. He wasn't good at this sort of thing and he knew it. He stood up and looked down the street at nothing in particular. Pat straightened out his legs and leaned back against the car.

"Why didn't you tell me that a long time ago? What kind of friend are you anyway?" Pat chuckled. Antonio looked down at his friend and offered him a helping hand.

"Let's go see if we can find any of those people you say must still be around. Maybe they can tell us what's good about this situation, if any."

"Sorry I wigged out on you man," said Pat. "Funny thing is, I thought you were the one who was about to do that a while back."

"Not enough time for both of us to do that," stated Antonio.

They continued using side streets and back roads until they found their way around the major fires and got back on the freeway north heading for Lodi. They rode mostly in silence though it was a more comfortable hush than on the earlier portion of their trip. The venting of feelings each in their own way has made them both more relaxed and at ease with themselves and each other. They seem more emotionally back on track and their resolve to find answers is definitely stronger. It may not be a perfect plan or the best, but they do have a plan, and until either of them comes up with a better one they will stick with it.

"There's a little truck stop just before we get into Lodi we used to eat at when we went deer hunting. It's almost noon and if you're as hungry as I am we might try stopping there for something to eat and a little R&R," recommended Pat.

"If your restaurant isn't char-broiled I think that is a good idea," declared Antonio. He was ready for a break and pulled over to let Pat take over the driving for a while.

Chapter 19

The heat was building as the day wore on. The earlier morning breeze seems to have dissipated. With no breeze coming from the ocean and reaching the inland valleys along with an inversion layer on top, it turned the central valley into a ready-made oven. The heat with no wind has lasted now for almost a week leaving the valley ripe with danger, a high fire hazard that local authorities have been warning everyone about since the week end, these are 'no burn' days, don't use gas powered lawn mowers and other gas power tools, no camp fires in the local parks and picnic areas, and of course watch where you throw those cigarette butts. Summer fires are bad enough to handle when there is someone around to fight them. Allowed to run rampant as now, they can be catastrophic for those left to deal with them.

Sitting in their air conditioned Pathfinder on the freeway heading north and dodging abandoned vehicles, Antonio and Pat were less concerned with fires at the moment, and more concerned with finding out whether or not the world had come to an end and left them to deal with it. Was that the ultimate rejection or what? While they had hoped to find some answers in places of authority they hadn't expected to find a lack of people, with authority or not, wherever they went.

Sacramento was their last hope of finding answers at an authoritative or governmental level. While they were now aware the likelihood of anyone being there was less than none they decided to stick with the plan. They didn't know what else to do. They haven't even planned where to go from there. That was too much to think about right now. First things first. The road sign they just passed on the right read Lodi 5 miles.

"Where's this fancy greasy spoon you're so keen on?" asked Antonio feeling hunger pains almost as sharp as other pains he's felt this morning, though not quite. This was physical; the others were emotional, mental, and psychological.

Pat broke out of his daydream to respond, "Not for a few miles yet. It'll show up on the right. There's a large tall sign you can see for a mile or so before you can read the damn thing, big sign, small letters. I think they wanted to keep you guessing till you got close enough to check it out."

"Well, I hope they don't open too early or the place may look like Betsy's right about now," exclaimed Antonio.

"Actually I believe they're open 24-7, but we've passed a few restaurants still standing in one piece," Pat replied. "We may have to cook our own meals. Somehow I don't think we'll find anyone begging to cook it for us. At least we can get it the way we want it."

"Like in the commercial, 'have it your way'," smirked Antonio.

"I've heard about that one but I haven't seen it yet," answered Pat. "Burger King isn't it?"

"Yea, I think so. One thing with our current situation though."

"Yea, what's that?" inquired Pat

"We don't have to leave a tip."

"Tip hell. We don't even have to pay for the meal. I mean, if we have to cook it ourselves, why should we pay for the damn thing?" Pat sat up and leaned forward, "There's the sign up ahead like I told you. And I don't see any smoke either."

"Maybe our luck is changing," joked Antonio. That would be nice he thought. Even on a small scale it would be a start. It was almost out of character for

Antonio to be thinking about luck. He never really believed in luck. Antonio always felt you made your own, good or bad, with the choices you make every day. If you wanted something to happen you make it happen yourself. You don't wait around on your backside for someone else to make it happen for you. That rarely ever happens he thought. Waiting could get to be a real habit. Problem is there are too many people waiting on other people to change their luck. Well, there used to be.

The large sign on the tall pole was close enough to be legible now. Antonio read Roadside Café. Good lord, how original he thought rather sarcastically. Couldn't they come up with something better than that? How 'bout Road Kill Café? May not be much more original but it would certainly grab your attention. After all, wasn't that the idea? Antonio suggested that to Pat.

"What?! Road Kill Café? Where the fuck did you come up with that one?" Pat was really taken aback and Antonio was shocked Pat had never heard of it. The bit was old and has been around for a long time.

"Pat, wouldn't you like to order a chunk of skunk or a slab of Lab?" Antonio asked.

"You're sick, man. I think this whole day has gotten to you," suggested Pat, but he couldn't help laughing at the whole idea.

Antonio kept it going, "How 'bout a smidgen of pigeon, or maybe some round of hound?" Pat was doubled over now. "Pat, I can't believe you never heard of this? Haven't you ever heard the phrase 'You kill it, we grill it'?"

"No man, where the hell did you come up with this shit?" Pat was truly amazed.

"It's been so long ago I don't even remember. Somebody showed me the whole menu once. It had a lot of other stuff on there I don't recall. Shit, we better pull off here." Pat pulled over to the off ramp and headed down to the right running the stop sign and parking in front of the restaurant entrance. He was blocking two cars in the handicapped spaces but was sure they wouldn't get any complaints.

There were a number of cars in the parking lot but all was very quiet. None of the usual restaurant sounds one would be familiar with approaching an eatery. Something they were getting use to now. Upon entering the restaurant they were hit immediately by the strong odor of burnt food and old smoke that hung in the air around the room, but no fire. What ever burned was contained in the kitchen. The café otherwise looked much the same as Betsy's when they walked in first thing this morning. There was cold food on the plates at the counter and on some of the tables, but no sign of confusion or panic.

"Let's find something to eat and get out of here," said Pat.

"Yea," was Antonio's only response. He headed for the kitchen and saw why the fire hadn't spread. Localized fire sprinklers had done their job and flooded the entire kitchen area.

"Shit," exclaimed Pat, "this is a fucking mess."

"Food in the refrigerator should still be good and all we need is one burner on the stove. Let's cook, eat, and run." Antonio was anxious to be done with this place. For some reason it made him uncomfortable. Pat found some bacon, ham, eggs, and in the freezer found the hash browns. Antonio cleared a large flat grill, turned it on, and had a burner next to it going by the time Pat brought the food over from the refrigerator. Being single and most experienced at it Pat cooked the meal. Antonio found dishes and utensils for them to use. Pat completed the culinary process and they brought their plates out to the dinning area.

"Where do you want to sit?" asked Pat.

"In the farthest seat from the kitchen to get as far away from that smell as we possibly can," said Antonio. They headed for a table in the far right corner of the restaurant. As they passed a table next to the window where a family of four had obviously been eating breakfast, something on the table lying next to a plate of half-eaten pancakes caught the corner of Antonio's eye and registered in his subconscious.

They continued to the corner table and sat down to eat. The odor was just as strong here as it was everywhere else in the room and did much to kill the taste of their food. They ate to curb their hunger but didn't enjoy it the way they might have under more normal circumstances. Pat's cooking wasn't that bad and it was a shame the quality was wasted in these conditions. Antonio ate most of his food but couldn't eat any more and threw his fork back over his right shoulder where it clattered across the table behind them and fell to the floor.

Surprised Pat gave him a funny look and said, "What the hell was that for?"

"I don't know, just always wanted to do it, now's my chance. You remember in those old movies about the middle ages where the people would eat a meal and toss the bones and utensils over their shoulders to the floor. They let the peons clean it up, or maybe nobody cleaned up. Maybe that's what started the black plague. You know, the filthy mess."

"You've got to stop this 'getting weird' on me shit," said Pat shaking his fork at Antonio. "We need to find some people so I can make a trade to replace you with somebody else. Preferably somebody in a skirt."

Pat's last remark only reminded him of Maria. He thought about how much nicer it would be if he were here eating breakfast with his wife and kids instead of Pat. Well, it was OK if Pat was there too, but he missed his family more than he could ever put into words. If there were any way he could go back and start things over like none of this ever happened he would spend more time with them doing things like this together. He remembers the last night he saw them and wishes he had been more positive with each of them. Antonio felt his most pleasant memory was helping Theresa get over her trouble with wearing the dress Maria had made for her.

He remembers walking into her bedroom and seeing her pretending to be reading a book similar to the one on the table by the window. Antonio sat up quickly in the seat startling Pat. "The book!" It was a diary. Before Pat could ask Antonio was out of his seat and running to the table where his subconscious recognized the diary lying next to the plate of pancakes. There it was. He reached over and grabbed the diary which was open and laying face down on the table. He turned it over and looked at the last entry. It was dated this morning.

Pat knew without asking that Antonio was checking out something that he'd seen probably on the way in. For some reason it didn't seem to mean any thing at the time but something clicked and off he went. He saw Antonio reading and waited for a response or reaction. It didn't take long.

"Oh, my God," said Antonio in utter amazement.

"What is it? What happened? What does it say?" Pat was anxious now.

"She saw something and had enough time to write this," said Antonio as he handed the diary to Pat. He grabbed the book and read quickly.

Date: June 7 – Day 3 of our vacation.

> Some vacation, all mom and dad
> do is argue. I think this trip is
> some last ditch effort to save
> their marriage. It isn't working.
> They think I don't understand. I
> understand better than they do.
> They need to start talking to
> each other instead of at each
> other. What's that sound? Some-
> thing is going on, everything
> is weird. I can see

"That's it? What the hell did she see?" Pat asked in bewilderment. He looked around almost expecting to see something maybe he hadn't noticed before. He saw nothing.

"I don't know," said Antonio softly. He too was looking around the restaurant though not to see what the diary's author might have seen, but wondering what's next. It's the first sign they've discovered of what happened to everybody. The first indication that people had at least some hint something was happening to them or something was changing right before their eyes. But what? They still had no clue. It didn't tell them what exactly became of everyone or where they went or how they went or even why. And why didn't they see it? Why are they the only two people left around to ponder this whole event, whatever it is? And are they really the only ones left? Will they still find people somewhere in their travels?

It was still impossible for them to surmise why they alone didn't know what was happening and why didn't it happen to them. Why didn't they hear anything out of the ordinary, or see whatever it was the little girl who wrote the diary saw? And which would make them better off, to have gone with everyone else wherever that is, or to be in their present situation?

Antonio searched the table and seats for more clues. He found a woman's purse. He opened it searching the contents and wondering why women carry so much junk in their purses. He found the woman's wallet pulling it out and tossing the purse to the table. Opening the wallet he saw the woman's driver's license. Her name was Sandra W. Anderson of Santa Monica, California. He hoped their trip wasn't going to last very much longer. Her license was going to expire next week.

"Anything there to help us?" asked Pat.

"No. Just the usual credit cards, a few receipts, family pictures, a couple of business cards. This one is for a lawyer." Antonio turned the card over. "A date and time written on the back. She must have had an appointment."

"Divorce lawyer?"

"Probably. From what the girl's diary said things weren't too cool between mom and dad. That kid sounded pretty bright. Most people don't give kids enough credit. There's nothing more in the wallet. Let's get out of here." Antonio was getting antsy now and wanted to be on their way. They walked out of the restaurant checking all the tables for any other papers or notes of any kind that someone else may have written while eating. It was a long shot but hey, they found the diary. What were the chances of that? They found nothing more, left the restaurant jumped into the car and headed back for the freeway. Maybe this was the right plan after all. They got their first clue, small as it was. That didn't mean they would find an answer, but it was a start. Their hopes were up.

Chapter 20

The trip north from the restaurant was marked by a sober silence. The hum of the engine and the drone of the tires on the asphalt road provided all the auditory stimulation available. Each of them swam in his own thoughts and Antonio believed he was going to drown in his. His head was spinning in a vortex of thoughts and images that kept coming at him faster than he could absorb. He couldn't get the statements in the diary out of his mind. The girl's entry in her diary actually created more questions than it answered, but they did have their first clue as to what happened. But what did it mean? Why didn't they hear the noise and what did she mean by everything being weird? How did knowing that much help them? What was next for them? They keep asking themselves the same questions over and over but they still can't come up with any answers. It didn't help them decide what to do next.

Sure, they were sticking with their plan to find help from official quarters even though neither one of them believed now they would find any. It's just that they don't know what else to do. But could their new found insight give them any clue as to where to go next, what to look for, or how to find it? Did knowing that everybody, well, for all they knew, most everybody, saw something coming, help them in any way know what was happening to them, or what to do about it? And why was it different for them? Why didn't they see or hear anything? They still had no answers.

Antonio feels like he's been looking for answers long before he started work this morning. The anxiety that he felt the last couple months he still believes was related to this whole event. He simply didn't have the ability to relate it, doesn't know what he could have done about it if he had. Trying to put the pieces together to solve the puzzle seems beyond his skills or ability and it's driving him crazy, driving him up the proverbial wall.

Times like now it all seems so hopeless and pointless, but he just can't give up, for Maria and the kid's sake if for no other reason. He has to know what happened, where are they, are they all right. He's made up his mind. If they can't find any answers in Sacramento, which now appears to be most likely, he simply wants to go back home regardless of conditions there. Where else? Home is still home. He's beginning to wonder if they ever should have left there in the first place. Maybe this whole trip was a mistake. But how could it be? If they hadn't come this way they never would have found the diary. Was this the beginning of finding answers to their mounting list of questions? Just thinking about it was driving him nuts.

Pat's thoughts were taking a different direction. He was still concerned about finding other people. The thought of them being all that is left continues to haunt him and scares him more than anything else. His whole life he has been alone and searching for someone or something to put it together and give him a feeling of belonging. He can not accept that it has come to this. He has to believe there are others who for whatever reasons have been left behind just as they were. The little girl's diary had mentioned three things that he keeps going over in his mind. What was the sound she heard, what was the weird feeling she experienced, and what did she see that caused her to abruptly end her entry?

Then of course the big question, what happened to her and her family, as well as the others in the restaurant? And what about these attacks on her senses? Why didn't he and Antonio notice any of those assaults on their senses? If everybody around them was affected why weren't they? Everyone in the homes in the neighborhood they were working must have heard it, felt it, seen it, so why not them? What's so different or special about them that they were left out?

Another thought occurred to Pat. They weren't the only people up that time of morning doing their job. What about nightshift crews in other types of work, you know, warehouse workers and shelf stockers who restock the stores over night? And what about grave yard shift people like taxi drivers and policemen, night watchmen and janitors and such? Did some of them make it through this thing? Did others not hear or see whatever it was? It only made sense to him that others slipped through this thing besides them. Pat's attention was diverted as they passed a road sign that read Walnut Grove Next Exit.

"Walnut Grove," he said aloud more to himself than to Antonio.

"Ever been there?" Antonio asked thinking Pat's remark meant he had some familiarity with the place.

"Never heard of it. I've heard of Walnut Creek, not Walnut Grove. Wonder how far off the road it is cause I sure don't see it," Pat observed. His voice seemed far off, almost dreamy.

"Don't see any smoke either," Antonio declared looking hard in all directions. He decided it was time to bring their thoughts in the open. "What do you make of the girl's diary?"

"I don't know," he said coming out of his trance. "I just can't understand how everybody else sees, hears, and feels something happening that we had not a clue what was going on," Pat said in consternation. He continued, "I still can't believe we're the only ones left. That doesn't make any sense."

"Hell, none of this makes any sense," agreed Antonio, "and frankly, I've stopped trying to make sense out of it. I just want to know what happened to Maria and Theresa and Ryan. If we don't find any answers in the capitol I'm going home. I think this was a mistake coming up this way."

"Hey, Antonio, it was your idea to make this trip. I went along with it because I didn't have any better idea at the time. But I think someone is telling us we did the right thing." Antonio looked at Pat quizzically. "If we hadn't stopped at that restaurant we wouldn't have found the diary," Pat added. "It may not have been much but it was a first clue."

"True, but a clue to what? We still really don't have any answers, just more questions."

"I can't get over the fact that with all the other swing and grave yard shift workers we can't find someone else besides us who came through this thing. There has to be others around," Pat said emphatically.

"You may be right, but if you know where to find them let me know. I'll be happy to go there. I could sure use some relief from your ugly mug," smiled Antonio.

"Up yours! We may not find governmental aid or anyone in authority to help sort this all out, but Sacramento is a pretty large city. If anybody came through this they might just gravitate to the capitol area. If we do find anyone else around to give us answers I'll bet that's where they will come from, not from the government," Pat suggested.

"On that I believe we can agree," Antonio admitted with a sigh. They sat in silence for awhile before Pat turned to Antonio.

"How much further, do you know?" he asked.

"About half an hour," answered Antonio, "we still haven't passed Elk Grove." Almost on queue they passed a road sign 'Elk Grove Blvd 1 Mile'.

"Speak of the devil," pointed Pat. "Damn, they're sure building out here." Pat observed the large construction effort of new homes going up just east of the freeway. He knew Antonio and Maria had started saving to buy a home but he could never see himself in that situation. He wasn't the family man type and besides, what did family ever do for him but cause him a lot of pain and heartbreak? He knew some people made a go of it, but he was afraid he wouldn't know how. He suddenly realized Antonio was talking to him.

"Yea, and a lot more in the planning stages from what I understand," said Antonio wondering if they'll ever get around to building it now. Antonio had to slow down a little as the abandoned vehicles were getting a bit thicker as they get closer to the capitol. He wondered how many plans large and small have been curtailed and whether any of them will ever be resumed, including his and Maria's. They had hoped to save enough to buy a real house with a back yard for family barbecues, planting gardens, a dog for Ryan, and maybe an above ground pool for the hot summers. They had almost half of their goal saved up in their special new home savings account. Maria wanted a gazebo with a hot tub in it for those cool nights when the kids were at grandma's and they could enjoy a romantic evening together. The apartment was nice, but it wasn't the American dream.

While it sounded good then it sounds even better now with the very real possibility that it may never happen looming over them. He knows now how much he had and only wishes he realized it then. Why do we have to lose something before we understand how much it means to us he thought? Why is it we can't take stock of what we have and realize what it all means before it is too late? He thinks about Maria's father and the pain that she went through when he passed away. Antonio thought he knew her suffering then but only now understands what she must have felt.

It may not be exactly the same; after all, she knew what happened then. He had lung cancer. Antonio has no clue what happened to his family, well, almost no clue. Some weird sound and weird feeling, described in a little girl's diary didn't provide much of a clue. This must be closer to what the families of missing children feel like. The worst part is the not knowing.

It's one thing to know that someone died of a heart attack, or cancer, or in a traffic accident, but for them to just vanish without a trace and not know what happened, it's worse than hell. How do you grieve? Are they dead?

Are they in a situation where they might be better off if they were dead? That's a hell of a thought. Parents of missing children must have nightmares about that every night. Only consolation for him Antonio thought was the fact that all the kidnappers and child molesters are gone too. Hey, there's a benefit to their present condition.

As they get closer to the capitol it is plain the sky over the city is dark and hazy. There isn't a cloud in the sky where they are so that means only one thing. Fires. The haze was no doubt smoke from buildings burning out of control. Antonio was trying to remember what off ramps they took to the capitol building when he rode on the school bus with Theresa's class field trip several months ago. He vaguely recalls J Street and was counting on that memory to get them there.

They were close enough now to the capitol to see their worst fears realized. The capitol was a raging inferno. Smoke was thick and widespread. The wind was blowing here and coming out of the northwest so the freeway was covered in smoke from the area known as Old Sacramento. This was not going to be easy, maybe even impossible. Between smoke and the freeway crowded with abandoned vehicles the going now was extremely slow. Reading overhead street signs was even becoming more difficult. They had to be careful they didn't get so lost they couldn't find their way back.

"Is it my imagination or is this more crowded with cars than what we've seen so far?" asked Pat looking around at the greater number of cars, big rigs, and delivery trucks. Antonio was having difficulty weaving in and out of the stranded maze of vehicles.

"I think there's plenty more, but I don't know if that's normal here, or if whatever happened came at a later time during the commute hours here then it did in the bay area. I just assumed it all happened at once. Maybe it didn't. Maybe it swept over the country like a wave or something, starting at one end and carrying everyone out in its wake as it crossed the country and around the globe," wondered Antonio.

Pat was thinking fast. Could that improve the chances that someone or some others were left behind just like they were? It seemed logical to him. Pat didn't think it strange for someone who was a staunch loner and one who feared commitment to a serious relationship would be the one ardently seeking out other survivors. Truth is it wasn't the commitment he was afraid of, it was the loss of it once attained that he feared. He wanted a real love and relationship so desperately, but growing up whenever he found it, it always seemed to let him down. He was afraid to lose again so he avoided the very thing he wanted most. With the world becoming an empty place it reminded him too much of his own solitary existence. Pat needed to find others to give himself the chance of finding what he most wanted, what we all want most, love of and for another human being. Now he fears it may be too late. He may never know.

"We need to get off this damn freeway," suggested Pat strongly.

"The surface streets may be worse, I really don't know. Watch for the J Street off ramp. I'm pretty sure that's the one we want to get to the capitol area." Antonio prays he remembers the right directions and that the way is not completely blocked off with traffic. It wouldn't be so bad if the cars were moving he thought, but then again, Antonio never had to drive miles and hours in normal commute traffic.

"Uh-oh. Did you know the freeway just split in a Y and we went to the left?" asked Pat.

"Through the smoke I didn't notice but if I remember right it's OK. I believe that's the way we want to go," Antonio prayed again. "Keep looking for the J Street exit." The farther they went the less sure he was of his directions. He slammed on the brakes squealing the tires and fishtailing the Pathfinder. A dark billow of smoke had blocked a delivery van from his sight and he almost slammed into it. As the smoke temporarily cleared they saw the overhead road sign which showed J Street was the next exit.

Antonio swerved to the right and headed for the exit, Pat felt relief that they were getting off the freeway finally. They didn't know if they were jumping out of the frying pan and into the fire but there was plenty of fire to go around. As they approached the side streets of the city the way was alternately clear or covered in smoke as the wind whirled past them with varying gusts of speed.

While the original plan for this trip was to seek aid and understanding about the current phenomenon from upper echelon government authority, neither of them expected any help from that quarter now. They did hope however to find other survivors, and through them, maybe some answers. The hope was the capitol being a large populated place and the capitol grounds with its park like setting and central location might draw survivors there. As they approach the area with the smoke, fires, and wind they wondered. Even that now was becoming increasingly doubtful also.

Chapter 21

If hell hath no fury like a woman scorned then Sacramento must be a woman someone badly scorned, spurned, insulted, and stomped on. The few buildings along J Street that weren't presently burning didn't have long to wait before flames would engulf them also. The heat, the cinders, the ash, and noise not to mention the smoke from the fires were more than Pat or Antonio could ever have imagined possible. They've never before been this close to a fire this far gone and their respect and admiration for all the former fire fighters who used to deal with these kinds of conflagrations grew enormously with every new fire they observed. It was more oppressive than anything either of them had ever experienced.

They theorized that with all the restaurants and hotel kitchens in the downtown area there were plenty of ignition sources for the fires to get a good hold within a very short time. Occasional explosions could be heard which they attributed to gas mains or transformers blowing up in various locations. They even began seeing burned out cars where burning debris from falling buildings had ignited gas tanks blowing them up also. Some of these streets could become more dangerous than they realized.

In some blocks vacant vehicles congested the road more than others so traveling down various streets fluctuated between smooth sailing and fighting the boulders through the rapids. They preferred the smooth sailing but now Antonio faced a huge boulder and came to a stop as the street in front of them was completely blocked from burnt out cars and fallen debris from a collapsed building still burning out of control. Antonio looked behind him as he put the car into reverse. He started backing up heading for the last cross street all the while keeping an eye on the building to their right which looked like it could fall any second and trap them in the middle of the block. The flames were the color of liquid gold and lined with brilliant reds and the heat was greater than his grandmother's ceramic kiln. The roar of burning buildings and furnishings forced them to shout at each other in order to be heard.

"Keep your eye on that building there. I don't like the looks of it," asked Antonio.

"I see it. Just hurry and I think we'll make it OK," said Pat optimistically. The building had a long front façade and was made up now of mostly flame, heat, and smoke. Antonio had just cleared the building when the rumble and shaking of the collapsing front wall caused the car to actually lift all four tires off the pavement as brick and glass from the five story structure crashed onto the road in front of them in a cloud of dust, smoke, ash, and debris. Flying pieces of brick, mortar, and glass pelted the front of the Pathfinder. A large piece of brick came flying toward them smashing the windshield creating a loud pop scaring the hell out of both men as the brick stuck in the windshield.

The ball of dust and smoke created from the collapsing wall pushed past them blinding the view of the street behind them requiring Antonio to navigate the rest of the block from memory. Fortunately for them this had been a smooth sailing block up to that point. Antonio only had two vehicles between them and the corner that he could remember and knew that they were close together facing the opposite direction. At that moment he grazed the first one breaking the right tail light on the Pathfinder and giving him only a split second to maneuver around the other vehicle which he managed to accomplish with about an inch to spare. They were at the corner of J and 5th Streets when Antonio came to an abrupt stop to catch his breath.

"That was too close," said Antonio wiping his brow.

"Going out as the main course in a barbecue is not my idea of how to end it," remarked Pat.

"I'm not ready yet to end it in any fashion. Help me clear this glass from the windshield," Antonio shouted as he started pushing the cracked safety glass out on the hood to clear his view. Pat started shoving glass out over the hood onto his side of the street. While they cleared out the cracked windshield they also allowed in the heat, smoke and stench from the outside into the vehicle. The smoke brought with it burnt ash which began to collect on everything.

"We'll need to find another car before we get out of here," Pat said.

"You think?" laughed Antonio as he turned the wheel and stepped on the gas. Without seeking an opinion from Pat, Antonio headed east along 5th Street hoping his memory from several months ago was still in tact. The wind and smoke was coming at them from behind now. Without a windshield he was glad they didn't have to drive into it. The smell and ash was bad enough the way they were going. Flying ash and soot was collecting on their clothing as well as the inside of the car now and the smell wasn't very pretty. They would need a change of clothing, not to mention a bath. They traveled several blocks when Pat started waving his hands.

"Hold on. Slow down. I thought I saw the capitol building through the smoke, over there," said Pat excitedly pointing to their left. Antonio came to a stop and stared while they waited for the winds to blow clear the view in that direction. It didn't take long as the winds were picking up speed and swirling smoke, ash, and flames in an ever-increasing firestorm. Antonio turned the wheel sharply left and floored the accelerator screeching past several cars abandoned in the lanes along Capitol Avenue.

As everywhere else they have been this morning the street up to the capitol building was empty of human or, for that matter, any other life form. The grounds around the capitol were also deserted. Antonio didn't hesitate to drive right over the curb across the lawn and up to the steps in front of the building. They jumped out of the vehicle and slowly climbed the steps to the front doors neither saying anything each knowing what the other was thinking. No one is here, no authority, no Governor, no legislators, no capitol police, no state troopers, no pages, no secretaries, no janitors. The whole trip was a waste of time. There is no help, aid, or explanation of what is happening coming from official sources because there are no official sources left.

While they had come to the conclusion this is what they would find long before they got here, seeing is believing, or not seeing as it were. In silence they went through the motions of checking the various offices and chambers finding no more here than they had anywhere else.

They looked through papers on desks and counters in hopes of finding other notes or writings that might give clues, as had the diary earlier in the day, but to no avail. They tried to find any office of emergency services or an emergency control center but couldn't find anything along those lines in the building. They were a little surprised having assumed that such a center for emergencies must exist somewhere in the complex. It was either located in an area not accessible to the general public, or located somewhere else in another building. They simply couldn't find it. In the end they came to the conclusion that at this point it no longer mattered anyway.

They were on the fourth floor in the office of an unknown state senator, at least to them, from somewhere in southern California realizing that they have run their course. Pat was finishing going through the papers on the senator's desk when Antonio came in from the outer office having completed the same chore on the desks of his secretary and other office staff. Antonio slumped down on large comfortably padded office chair.

"Nothing there," he said for what seemed like the hundredth time this afternoon.

"Here either," replied Pat as he stared at Antonio's soiled form slumped in the overly ornate chair. "You're going to get that fancy chair filthy. The tax payers will be angry."

"That's OK. My taxes paid for this chair and probably a few more like it. I'll get it as dirty as I want." He paused. "So this is it," stated Antonio. It was not a question. He was emotionally exhausted and feeling more drained than he could ever remember having felt before. Pat walked away from the desk and looked out the window at the raging fires below burning what used to be the capitol city of the fair state of California. Look at it now. In a matter of a few days after all the fires have fed on what fuel was left there would be nothing but the charred cinders of the heart of a people. California, the economic heart of a great nation that for over 200 years was the leader of the free world. So what did it all mean? Did any of this ever have a purpose? What point did our puny existence have anyway? Was it all for naught now that it is all gone? Pat felt empty, lost, and lonelier than ever before in his lonely miserable life. What was it all for?

The last time Pat felt this lost was when he was 11 years old and got separated from Uncle Mike on a hunting trip in the foothills east of Sonora. They had stopped for dinner the night before in Jamestown and drove till dark to a place where Uncle Mike frequented off the beaten path and off limits for hunting but Uncle Mike never let that stop him. He knew the area and how to avoid the game wardens and park rangers. They were hunting with bows and arrows so the noise of gun shots wouldn't give them away and he wanted to get close enough to the deer to allow Pat a real shot at bagging a buck. Believing this was the only way to avoid dangerously careless hunters and competition for the deer was how he justified it.

They spent the night sleeping in the back of Mike's truck and struck out early on a trail Mike found of fresh deer tracks. They split up on each side of a small knoll when somehow Pat wandered a bit too far wide and couldn't find his way back. Mike spent the better part of the day kicking himself for letting Pat out of his sight and trying to track Pat hoping not to need outside help to find him, but knowing he must if it meant the difference. He wouldn't take the chance of not finding his nephew. For Pat's part he walked around frightened and lost for several hours alternately crying and trying to put on a brave face by wiping his tears trying to act like a grown up. Finally he sat down and tried to remember the things Uncle Mike taught him about survival.

He never thought much about it when Uncle Mike was teaching him. Pat figured he would never get lost, not with Uncle Mike around to protect him. Now that it actually happened, he tried very hard to remember everything that he was taught. He tried to look for existing trails but this far off the beaten path there weren't any. He looked and listened for a river or a road for sounds of water or traffic. Pat didn't remember crossing any creeks or seeing any rivers but tried to think real hard which way the road was they turned off of earlier that morning. The sun had been in front and a little to their right when they pulled off the road and parked behind some trees. Uncle Mike then led the way north from the road. That means if he walked straight south he should logically run into the road sooner or later. He started walking.

He walked for what seemed like forever to an eleven-year-old but was actually about forty minutes. As luck would have it he came upon the two-lane highway and was standing there for several minutes when he saw a truck coming from the east heading in his direction. As the truck approached he recognized Uncle Mike who drove up and pulled in front of him.

Mike had finally decided to go for help and was driving back to the nearest camp ground when he spotted Pat coming out of the trees. They both forgot their macho though guy thing and began crying in each other's arms. They realized how lucky they were and how much worse it could have turned out. Uncle Mike never took chances like that again. He planned future excursions with more people or simpler tracks that made it possible to keep Pat in sight at all times. He also gave Pat a whistle to use next time just in case.

While it turned out well, Pat had never known that kind of fear and loneliness before or since, not until now. This time there was no Uncle Mike to pull over and take them back to civilization. This time they were on their own to find where they were going and how to get there. Antonio was watching Pat at the window wondering what he was thinking but too exhausted to ask. As Pat finally turned toward him Antonio rose from the pretentious chair.

"Not one single solitary soul walking around down there," Pat said solemnly. "If anyone were still around in this inferno you'd think this is one place they'd come. The building's not on fire and there is some green grass, open space and for now at least some water."

"Let's go home," Antonio murmured quietly.

"Good idea, but from what I can see out there it may not be so easy leaving the area," commented Pat.

"We'll find our way through. It's still early afternoon. We'll be in Dublin before dinner," Antonio bragged. The word dinner didn't seem to have the same connotation it had before. As they headed out the building they knew there was no one home to prepare a nice home cooked meal, that most if not all the restaurants, fast foods, and other eating establishments were in all likelihood well done themselves by now. The world wasn't the same. Question now was would it ever be the same again?

Chapter 22

The trip out of the capitol was much the same as running a mouse through a gauntlet filled maze. Clouds of billowing smoke churned by gusty winds hampered them every inch of the way blinding and choking them as they went. Vacant and abandoned vehicles were not the only encumbrances that had to be circumvented in this obstacle course that was once the streets and thoroughfares of a vibrant capitol city. Fallen buildings and wind blown debris from the massive firestorm made things impossible in some blocks and merely a formidable challenge in the rest. With some backtracking lucky guessing and a will to escape they managed to be headed south on I-5 in only twice the time they had expected. By this time they considered themselves fortunate to have gotten out at all.

"I feel like we've inhaled enough smoke to make up for not smoking cigarettes the last ten years," complained Antonio as he coughed up soot from his throat and spit out the window. “God what a mess,” he said referring to the city and the phlegm.

“The first motel we see let’s stop and get cleaned up and see if we can’t find another car,” said Pat. “We look like hell, stink like shit, and this thing that passes for a car is a rolling disaster. This thing is still under warranty isn’t it?”

“Well, you don’t look or smell any different than you normally do, and I believe the warranty is only good if you paid for the vehicle. But, do you think they might give us much for a trade in?” joked Antonio, though they tried hard to break the grip fatigue held them in, they weren’t really in a joking mood now, too exhausted to laugh and too tired to smile. Pat just leaned his head back and looked up at the car ceiling. He quickly closed his eyes as soot and ash collected there would fall into his eyes whenever they hit a bump or rough spot in the road. He couldn’t wait to wash this crap off and find a change of clothes; they didn’t even have to fit. Anything was better as long as they were clean. They were used to dirty stinking clothes collecting garbage for a living, but this was different. The odor was the burnt failure of a city or a civilization to defend itself from a final conflagration. It was more than soot and ash; it represented the end of all they had ever known.

Antonio sensed Pat wasn't as relaxed as he was letting on. He has known Pat for over eighteen years and it seems to him that his partner is more tense then usual even for the circumstances they were in. Pat was not one who could hold his emotions in check. He usually wore them right out there on his sleeve where everyone could see them. Antonio has had to bail Pat out of more than one jam because of it. But now Pat seemed to be holding back. This was highly unusual and Antonio was worried about his friend. As if he didn't have enough to worry about looking for his family, now it appeared Pat may be emotionally disintegrating.

Antonio headed south and kept an eye out for a motel or tourist rest area, anywhere they might find a shower and another vehicle. Anything with keys in it, or at least lying somewhere near by, otherwise they would have to hot wire it. That would be no big deal and an easy job for Pat. He was the one with that kind of knowledge and experience. A motel of course was preferable as car keys may still be in the room for vehicles in the parking lot.

He wondered if it was possible to search the rooms not just for the keys, but maybe find another written clue left behind by someone the same way the little girl left her diary in the restaurant. Sure it was a long shot, but so was finding the diary on the table. What were the odds of that?

People sometimes wrote journals and diaries while on trips. It might be worth looking for, and if they didn't find anything, the only thing lost was a little time. They seem to have plenty of that. Unless of course whoever is responsible for this whole disappearing act suddenly remembers, 'Oops, we forgot these two' and comes back to retrieve the missing duo. He didn't care for that idea at all. He couldn't think of any scenario that would fit their present circumstance. Try as he might he just can't make any sense of everything that has happened to them. Damn, thought Antonio, here I go thinking too much again.

"Keep your eyes on the road, dummy," he said to himself.

It wasn't long before he spotted several motels located together on the right side of the freeway with several fast food restaurants. Two of the eateries were smoldering ruins. A Carl's Jr. was still in tact and a

Comfort Inn was next door also untouched yet by fire. He took the nearest off ramp and headed for the motel. Antonio parked in front of the lobby and they both jumped out trying in vain to brush off the filth from their clothes.

"Damn, this shit just doesn't want to come off," said Antonio in frustration. A condition they've become all too familiar with. Frustration and anxiety seemed to be the order of the day. It was taking a toll on both of them.

"Ah, who's gonna care, lets just go in?" said Pat conceding defeat.

Antonio laughed, "Yea, really. Let's grab a room and a shower."

"Bullshit. You find your own room. I ain't taking no shower with you," cried Pat in mock disbelief.

"You stupid moron," said Antonio shaking his head.

"Up yours," replied Pat with his favorite comeback.

They tried reverting back to their usual more casual manner due mostly to the relief of getting out of the inferno and imminent opportunity to refresh themselves with a shower and meal. But it felt forced and even contrived. The light banter and tomfoolery that normally filled their daily interaction didn't have the same feel; it lacked the humor and congeniality, and even the casual spontaneity they were used to. Inside the lobby Pat went behind the registration desk and took keys for two rooms next to each other on the second floor. He tossed one set over to Antonio.

"Carry your own bags, the bellhop is on strike," he reported somberly as he headed out from behind the desk.

"Wait a minute. If these keys are in there then these are empty rooms," remarked Antonio.

Pat gave him a funny look and answered, "Antonio, I believe we'll find they're all empty, unless you know something I don't."

"No. I mean they were empty when all this started. The other rooms had people in them and there would be clean clothes we could change in to. We need a set of master keys that will open all the rooms." Antonio started back behind the registration desk.

"Look for the maid's keys. They have to open all the rooms to clean them, right?" replied Pat.

"Yea, but would they keep them here with the guest's keys?" asked Antonio believing he wouldn't find any employee keys here.

Pat thought a minute, “I think you’re right. There must be an employee room where they would report for work, pick up their cleaning carts, and their room keys. But where?” Pat was standing at the far end of the lobby where he noticed a door to the right of and behind the registration area with a small sign above it that read ‘Employees Only’.

“Here,” he yelled and hurried to the door in a kind of forced trot. Running was a bit much to expect in their current exhausted condition. Antonio followed as they entered a hall with what appeared to be a break room on the right, a supervisor’s office on the left. Pat entered the office while Antonio went on down the hall where there were more doors to inspect. The next one on the right turned out to be a large storage area where the cleaning carts were lined up for the next days work. It’s anybody’s guess when that will be. He found a set of keys on the third cart he searched.

“Yes,” he exclaimed.

About the time he turned around Pat came dashing through the door also holding a set of keys he’d found in the supervisor’s desk. They looked and smiled at each other holding their respective key sets. Antonio spoke first.

"Let's get upstairs and hope the place wasn't reserved for a women's convention. You'd look real cute in a pink chiffon dress," he chuckled.

"You've been away from Maria too long," replied Pat regretting his words as soon as he said them. It was too late to take them back now. He wasn't sure how Antonio would respond and was a little uneasy as he waited. Antonio's smile left his face as a mask of heartache replaced it. His soul heavy with grief at the reminder of what he's lost. Antonio looked at his friend knowing Pat would never understand the loss or the pain.

"You're right," was all he said and Antonio quietly left the room heading back to the lobby.

Pat slowly followed wanting to kick himself in the ass for the stupid remark but knew there was nothing he could do about it now. They headed for the elevators and went up to the second floor and started opening doors looking for rooms with clothes left behind by recently evaporated guests hoping each could find something that came at least close to fitting. Both were within an inch of six feet tall Pat being the taller of the two but neither far from average height. Finding clothes to fit didn't seem like a daunting problem but it wasn't till they reached the third floor and running out of rooms before they found clothes that worked for them both. They took separate rooms to clean up and change and each entered without another word between them.

Antonio searched the room for any signs of handwritten material or other visual indications of what happened to everyone. He found no letters, diaries, or journals of any kind. A newspaper that was two days old lay on the floor and a recent news magazine on the chair near the television was open to a story about the Eastern European troubles. Light reading for an early wake up call. One briefcase on the bed was full of brochures for cleaning products announcing a new line of liquid hand soaps for the man or woman working with grease or oils that were unusually hard to remove. He looked at himself in the mirror and thought he could use some of that right about now.

Enough of this, it was time for him to clean up. I'll stick to regular hotel bar soap he thought as he tossed the brochures on the bed. He found the man's electric shaver and other toiletries and proceeded to shower, shave, and change. All the while he didn't know whether to ask Pat to help him look for clues in a room to room search or just do it on his own. He wasn't sure how Pat would respond. He has noticed a slow but sure pattern of behavior that has him worried about Pat's mental or emotional handling of their situation. He's decided to just play it by ear.

Looking in the mirror feeling fresher but still seeing the undercurrent layer of exhaustion reminding him what they've been through and what must still be done. His eyes were bloodshot and red, his face drawn and taut, and his heart pained. How he would love to just climb into one of the beds and forget everything and if it weren't for the need to keep up the search for Maria and the kids he would have done just that.

Antonio still wasn't sure which was the right decision at this time; look for clues as to what happened to everyone and by virtue of that learn what happened to his family, or simply go home and continue the earlier search for them directly. His worst fear was to find out too late that he made the wrong choice. He didn't take long to make up his mind. He was here now and wanted to make the most of it.

A room to room search wouldn't take too long he thought as long as he was quick and methodical. He would start on his own and as soon as Pat realized what he was doing Antonio counted on Pat joining him in the search. The Inn was three stories high and about twenty rooms per floor. Antonio tried some quick mental math. If he spent five minutes per room he soon realized it would take much longer than he expected, about five hours. With both of them searching and cutting the time in half it was still too long. He really didn't want to spend that much time off the road and feared reaching Dublin after dark. If he enlisted Pat's help from the start, and only spent two minutes per room, they could be done in closer to an hour. That was better and doable. He had no choice. Pat had to be brought in from the start.

After knocking on the door to Pat's room he waited several minutes before the door opened. Antonio gave his friend a quick once over before Pat walked back into the room without saying a word. Antonio entered a bit apprehensively. Pat was cleaned up and dressed but didn't appear in much better condition than he was earlier. He was tense and his movements quick and jerky, not so much as anyone who didn't know him would notice, but enough for Antonio to be concerned. Not being able to predict Pat's reaction he decided to be straight forward and up front about it.

"I want to make a quick search of all the rooms."

Pat shot him a glance like he was out of his mind.

"If we work together and spend no more than two minutes in each room we can do it in an hour."

"Why? What's the point? What the hell are we looking for?" questioned Pat.

"Anything that might give us a clue as to what happened. When we come across an empty room that gives us a little more time in a room with more to look through. We look for letters, journals, diaries, anything that might help like the little girl's diary this morning."

"Get real Antonio. Do you have any idea what the chances are of finding anything like that? We're just wasting a lot of time for nothing. This is bullshit, man," complained Pat as he threw his towel on the chair next to the dresser.

"OK. I admit it's a long shot, but please humor me on this if nothing else. Finding the diary was a long shot this morning. You're right; we may find nothing, but what if we do find something? It's possible. Look, people on trips write letters and journals and stuff. It's worth a shot Pat especially if we get even part of an answer. Work with me on this please," he pleaded. Pat wasn't convinced but relented.

"All right, at least the building isn't on fire, yet. I still think this is a fucking waste of time." Pat shook his head and grabbed his master key and headed for the door.

Antonio detected a kind of defeatist attitude in Pat's voice. He was still concerned about his friend's state of being and wondered how much he could depend on him from now on. They needed each other and Antonio was afraid how he would handle things if Pat really lost it. Maybe the activity of looking for clues would help him get back on track. He hoped so.

"You cover the second floor. I'll go up and cover the third floor. When we're done we can both cover the first floor together and then head home," said Antonio. He waited for a response from Pat as his friend went out the door.

"Shit," was all Pat had to say.

Chapter 23

Time ceased to have any meaning. What seemed like hours turned in to minutes. Earlier in the day minutes of terror felt like an eternity. The lack of consistency in time was as aggravating as everything else they had to contend with. Antonio hasn't worn a watch in over ten years, but not being able to accurately gauge the time he spent searching each room was bothering him. He picked one up from a table in a room on the third floor. True or not, he felt as though he was moving faster once he could properly time himself. He realized it was probably all in his head but if it worked, what the hell, go with it. Psychologically he felt as though he were moving faster.

Antonio was worried about how Pat was doing but couldn't break away from the task at hand to check on him. He really believed that if there was anyplace they could find anything even close to the diary in terms of providing information it would be in a location like this. Where else could this many people be in one place at one time and have even the slimmest chance of leaving behind some kind of written clue. If it was going to be anywhere this was the place.

Antonio was not only more enthusiastic, but quite thorough as he was absolutely certain they could find a clue here if they only looked in the right places. He could not believe this many people in one spot at one time wouldn't at least inadvertently leave some message behind. The thought hit him that he was like an archeologist looking for clues as to how people lived, looking for messages left behind, except he wasn't waiting hundreds or thousands of years, not even days. His biggest problem was not being able to spend more time in each room. He felt rushed, hurried, and not able to be as thorough as he would like.

Antonio searched each room with a methodical effort, hoping to be as complete and rapid as possible and get through the search as quickly as he could. As he completed more rooms he was becoming disappointed at not finding what he was looking for. He was so sure they could find something. He began to wonder if it wasn't just wishful thinking. That thought he pushed from his mind as soon as it appeared.

New thoughts and feelings grew in his mind; similar to those that began months ago when this all started for him. He was now sensing an urgency he hadn't felt before as if time was becoming an issue. Again it was nothing he could point to, nothing he could put a finger on, just a compelling sense that there was a limited time to finding an answer before it was too late. That thought made him freeze, too late for what? Fear of the unknown was more than just a phrase. It was a reality when things around were happening that you have no control over, were affecting your life, your very existence, and it seems you can't do a damn thing about it. You grasp at straws and claw your way through by doing whatever it takes to regain some control over your own destiny. For Antonio searching the rooms for some hint as to what was going on was his own meager attempt at doing that. Even the smallest clue would make this effort all worth while and give him a sense of being back in the driver's seat.

Unfortunately he knows Pat wasn't being as complete in his search of the rooms. He didn't have to be with him to know that. It was Pat's attitude toward the whole enterprise. Antonio was aware Pat didn't think much of the search effort. He couldn't get through to Pat how sure he was about this and how important he felt this was to finding an answer, and with an answer, finding what happened to Maria and the kids. The whole point of leaving Dublin was to find out what happened to everybody and by virtue of that he would also discover what happened to his family. Finding no trace of anyone least of all his family has been disheartening and frustrating. That was another reason for keeping busy looking for an answer anyway he could. The busier he kept himself, the less he thought about his family. Damn it Antonio stop thinking and get on with the search.

The former occupant of this room must have been a pretty boring guy, no cigarettes, no booze, no dirty magazines or books, no family pictures, no exciting clothes, expensive, but not exciting, just plain dark solid color shirts and dark pants. This guy was as plain as you can get he thought. What Antonio didn't know was the man whose room he was searching was an undercover D.E.A. agent on assignment. Being able to blend in unobserved and unidentified was a required attribute. The last thing he wanted was to be noticed. The agent was investigating a drug ring in Sacramento and had only been here for three days. The drug agent's clothes may be expensive, but they were too small for Antonio anyway. Too bad he thought, not that he had any place to dress up for now.

On the floor below Pat walked into the room as he removed the key from the lock. He's covered some fifteen rooms on this floor and thinks he's wasting his time. The room is similar to all the rest, long and narrow with two twin beds coming from the right or left wall in alternating order. An open closet on the left with some men's sports clothes hanging from the rack. A small suitcase or oversized briefcase, it could be either, lay on a portable rack. Pat couldn't understand why they designed cases like that. It was like the designer couldn't make up his mind what he wanted, briefcase or suitcase. He was probably a fagot too, Pat thought. After all, only women and faggots became dancers or designers, right?

He also couldn't figure out what he was doing here. He passed up the case without opening it and walked around the bed to the table by the window. They are not going to find another diary and they could be on their way home instead of wasting their time on this wild goose chase. Besides, what if they did find a note or letter and someone else writes what the little girl wrote, weird feeling, weird noise, and whatever else? What would that prove? Would they know anymore than they do now? Pat looked around the room quickly seeing no diary, no letter, and no written materials of any kind lying in the open. He's not surprised. The thought of going through desk and dresser drawers occurs to him but he dismisses the idea, just more waste of time. He did that in the first ten or twelve rooms or so but has no enthusiasm for it and doesn't even want to go through the motions anymore.

Pat turns and heads for the door passing the space between the beds on his way. On the floor near the nightstand are a camera case and a video recorder. He catches sight of it as he continues on but it makes no impression on him. It may have been of interest to him in the past but he has nothing or no one to take pictures of now. Not that he ever did. What Pat failed to notice was the red LED on the video recorder was on. The camera's owner was trying out his new recorder and was taping at the time of the event.

He was a salesman returning home after a more than successful sales trip and bought the recorder as a surprise for his wife. He knew she wanted one to record their new baby as he went through the growing stages of first word, first step, first birthday and all the other firsts of going from infant to toddler. She knew they really couldn't afford one but it was her small dream.

With this successful trip he felt proud that he could make this little dream of hers come true. He had the camera out and was going over all the features so he could show her everything it could do when he brought it home. Then strange things began to happen around him. He dropped the camera on the floor where it lay taping everything that transpired. Pat continued out the door closing it behind him.

The afternoon dragged on warm and muggy the smoke from not so distant fires filling the horizon with surreal smog like haze. The sun barely shone through casting an eerie pinkish-purple light on the world below. The general atmosphere created a claustrophobic feeling that seemed to affect Pat more than it did Antonio. Pat was ready to start skipping rooms in an effort to be done with the whole effort and get back on the road. It wasn't that he had anything or anyone to get back to; it was more to do with a feeling of being trapped in one place not knowing what was going on. He needed to be on the move going someplace, anyplace, it didn't matter where.

His whole life seemed to be an attempt to get somewhere. He just never had a clue as to where he was supposed to be going or why. There were times he envied Antonio for having a family to go home to with a wife and kids who loved and cared for him and he caring for them in return. It was something he never knew and missed more deeply than he ever let on. His childhood experiences weighed heavily on him though he tried to deny it, mostly to himself. Pat never seemed to learn that receiving the caring and love he always wanted begins with being able to give the same. And to be able to do that means first caring about ones self.

Antonio is leaving a room on the third floor when he sees Pat coming out of the elevator. If he was worried before he's frightened now. Pat looked liked something that crawled out of one of their garbage trucks on a hot humid summer afternoon. The ash and soot may have been washed away but the fear, fatigue, and exhaustion in him has magnified ten fold. Pat stepped away from the elevator and looked both ways before he spotted Antonio.

"Let's get the fuck out of here, man. We're wasting our time with this shit." His voice wasn't slurred but it sounded tired, resigned. There was no life in it. All hope has gone out of him and despair is all that is left. Antonio wanted to finish the job as they were almost done.

Antonio chose his words carefully, "Alright, I think you may be right. I only have three more rooms left. I'll just finish up here and meet you down in the restaurant." Pat grunted and headed back down the elevator.

Antonio is resigned now to skipping the search of the first floor rooms. He hates to give it up but he can't risk antagonizing Pat anymore for fear of having a mutiny on his hands. There are fewer rooms on the ground level so it's not as big a loss as it could have been. Of course, Murphy's Law says that's where a clue will be if there is one here to be found. Entering the next room Antonio is beginning to wonder if this was really worth the effort. They've gained nothing and lost some valuable time. He started second guessing himself wondering if he really believed they would find something in the way of a clue as to what was going on, or if it was all just wishful thinking. In the last three rooms he found only a letter home on the desk in the last room. It stopped in mid-sentence but gave no hint as to why. The pen lay on the page as if placed there by the author as he got up to check on something.

"Damn," thought Antonio.

Still feeling it had been worth the effort despite the negative outcome Antonio headed down the hall to the elevator to join Pat in the fast food restaurant below. As the elevator dropped toward the first floor Antonio couldn't help but feel they missed something. He just doesn't know what or how. He was so sure an answer was here.

Well, he thought, life goes on. It's time to plan our trip home and where to go and what to do next. He's not sure how to handle Pat and his seeming emotional decline. Antonio knows he can't do it alone. He needs Pat's help but he also needs Pat to be one hundred percent, or at least close to it. The door opens and he walks out toward the restaurant. He sees Pat standing in the middle of the dining area looking around at the counter and tables. Antonio senses something is not right. He walks in and begins surveying the area as he walks up to Pat. Pat turns to look at him, "You notice anything different?"

Still looking over the scene before them Antonio answers, "Yea, there are no half eaten meals or half empty cups on any of the tables, or the counter either. The lights are all on. What do you make of it?"

"I think it happened after the morning crew got in but before they opened," replied Pat.

"That would make sense except these kinds of places are usually open 24 hours," observed Antonio.

Pat walks behind the counter and heads into the kitchen. He looks at the stoves and grill. "Nobody was cooking anything," he yells back to Antonio. "The grill's not even turned on."

"That's probably why this place didn't burn," Antonio hollered back. "But why? What was different here," Antonio wondered aloud?

"Who cares Antonio? Let's just get something to eat and get the hell out of here, ok," Pat insisted loudly. "We're not going to find any damn diaries in here." He turned around and headed back behind the counter. There he found a cherry pie, placed it on the counter and grabbed a fork. He stabbed the pie with the fork and began eating. "I don't think anybody will mind if I eat it this way," he said with a grunt.

Antonio chuckled and agreed. He headed back to the kitchen looking for something more substantial to eat. In the refrigerator he found some pre-cut slices of sandwich meat, lettuce, sliced tomatoes and condiments. He pulled out what he needed and made several sandwiches, one for now and some for the road. He bagged the road sandwiches and grabbed a soda. Joining Pat at the counter he offered Pat a sandwich.

"That's quite alright, this will do me just fine," he said with a mouth full of pie. Pat had a milk he got from the cooler behind the counter. The pie was half gone. That made Antonio feel better. If Pat still has an appetite he can't be too far gone. It may not be the healthiest of meals but at least he was eating something.

"Let's hurry up here and grab some supplies from the kitchen and get moving. I think you're right. We need to get home."

"Why", questioned Pat? "What's there? Besides, how we gonna get there?" He looked Antonio straight in the eye. Antonio saw resignation remained in Pat's eyes.

"Oh, shit. I forgot. We still need to find another vehicle." Antonio dropped his sandwich and headed for the parking lot. He started going from car to car looking for keys someone might have left in the ignition. After a fruitless search he headed back for the motel entrance where Pat was waiting for him.

"You really didn't think you were going to find any did you?" Pat queried.

"Well, it was worth a shot," said Antonio.

"There's another Pathfinder parked over there in slot marked for room 114. Let's check that room for keys," suggested Pat.

"Good thinking. Keep it up old buddy," replied Antonio.

Pat wasn't sure how to take that last remark but was in too much of a hurry to get out of here to worry about it now. They entered room 114 and began searching pants pockets and drawers. "Found them," shouted Antonio as he slammed closed the night stand draw and headed out the door.

They went back into the restaurant to grab their sandwiches and a few other items for the trip and headed for the on ramp south. They left the soot covered gear in the old Pathfinder as they could replace it all when they got back to Dublin. Antonio was driving and didn't hold back. He hit over ninety and dared the CHP to stop him. In fact, he wished they would. Though he knew that was highly unlikely he still couldn't believe that they were the only two left alive. That just didn't make any sense. What would that accomplish? If some higher power wanted to start over this was obviously an unlikely scenario. Maybe there are two women wondering around like them just waiting for the right time and place to meet. Yea, right. Antonio started wondering if he was losing it.

Chapter 24

The trip south was a combination of excitement and desperation. Antonio was excited about heading home and continuing the search for his family. He couldn't give up hope that somehow he would still find them alive and well. When, where, and in what condition were still the big questions. Thinking about what his family was going through, and what they needed to do to survive was an area he tried to stay away from. It made him uncomfortable to consider the more difficult problems they must be facing. He hoped that fear and paranoia didn't prevent them from seeking food, shelter, and other necessities, as well as looking for help. He feared they were having no more luck finding survivors than they were having. Finding them was paramount now. No more wild goose chases seeking help from anyone. They were on their own and had to deal with things on that level.

It made sense that he would need a plan, an organized course of action that would make the process of finding them quick and thorough. Thorough was the most important as he didn't want to overlook an area only to miss them by being too hasty or careless. The thought of never seeing them again haunts him like an unending nightmare. Antonio only hoped that the time spent looking for help from higher authority hasn't cost them any chance of finding Maria and the kids.

He was also desperate as the feeling of time becoming an issue was growing stronger. He ignored these feelings before, months ago when this all started for him. He didn't want to make that mistake again. There was no more understanding now of what the feelings and premonitions all meant, no more than before, but he intended to pay attention to them now. How he would do that he still wasn't sure, but he wasn't going to ignore them either.

He also promised Pat not to leave him out of the loop, keeping such feelings to himself, not sharing them. Antonio glanced over at Pat. He cringed a little. Pat's attitude and overall morose behavior has become a problem for Antonio and he was still unsure of how to handle the situation. He really wanted and needed Pat's help and companionship. They have been friends for a long time and trying to handle things without his help was unimaginable. As far as they knew, there was no one else. Unless they succeeded in finding anybody, they were all either of them had left.

"Pat, when we get back to Dublin, you know I'm going to need your help trying to find Maria and the kids. We need a plan to work from so we don't waste a lot of time. You with me pal?" He looked over at Pat waiting for a response.

Pat hesitated then slowly turned his head in Antonio's direction. "You really think we're going to find them after all of this," he asked sullenly. "I really don't mean to be cruel but I hate to tell you man, it ain't going to happen."

"Pat. You don't think I could give up on them do you? I can't give up. Come on man, I need your help," Antonio insisted.

Pat sighed and gave a small shrug of his shoulders. "You got my help if only because there really isn't any thing else to do, you know. I feel for you man, but you got to be realistic. They're gone, just like everybody else."

"I can't accept that. I don't believe that. I'm not giving up. With you or without you I'm continuing the search. I really need your help. Don't give up on me Pat. Come on, man," Antonio pleaded.

"I told you, you got it. But sooner or later we're going to have to decide how we're going on, just the two of us from what I can see. We will have to survive on that basis, for whatever it's worth. There ain't nobody else," Pat was firmly convinced now that for whatever reason, they were all that was left. They were not going to find Maria, the kids, or anyone else. Some how the world ended and they were left out, or behind, or something. Who the hell cares? What's done is done and they need to go on. This business of searching for anyone is just a waste of fuckin' time, he thought.

Antonio didn't respond. He didn't want to get into an argument about the future beyond searching for his family at this point. He realized that the time may come when the decision to give up on the search may become a reality. Until then, he wasn't thinking about it. Only one thing was occupying his thoughts for now. It is all that gives what's left of his life any meaning.

The realization of that finally hits him. If they don't find Maria, if they don't find anyone, that means the two of them are all that's left. If that is the case, then even if they lived out full natural lives, once they die off, it's over. No more human race. It just can't be thought Antonio. Even if they never find Maria, they would have to find females somewhere or the species is gone. The finality of it all strikes home. Until now they were looking for someone else in the belief that others must have survived if only in small pockets of two or three just as they had.

Without realizing it Antonio had let up on the accelerator a bit slowing the vehicle. Pat noticed and asked, "What's wrong?" as he looked around for something out of the ordinary, well, out of the new ordinary. Antonio snapped out of his train of thought long enough to speed up again.

"Sorry, man. I was carried away thinking of how to start the search when we got back home. Just wasn't paying attention," he lied. Pat was skeptical but let it pass as they were back at high speed again. That was all he cared about. Get back to familiar ground. Pat could think of nothing else now. From there he could handle the future with a little more comfort. He would help his friend look for his family for a while, but after that, he didn't know. He would wait and see what the situation looked like at that time then decide for himself what would be the best action to take in his own best interest.

Antonio decided to change the subject of his thoughts. It was all getting too deep for him. Heavy thinking was never his favorite past time. He decided to concentrate on the world around him, although it was almost as depressing. Some residential areas had scattered fires or burned out homes. The business districts were harder hit, especially those with fast food restaurants or other all night eateries near by.

The smoke and haze from multiple fire sources fills the air with acrid smelling fumes most the trip with only few and far between more rural less inhabited areas with more breathable air. The morning breezes had ceased along this section of the valley and the hot sun baked the acrid air into a stifling stench that assaulted their nostrils. Antonio had retied the scarf around his face so he looked like a highway robber of old. It really didn't help but it made him feel better.

As they passed through Tracy on 205 heading for the Altamont Pass Antonio became apprehensive. Areas of Tracy were burned out while others looked like a modern ghost town; empty, still, devoid of any life big or small. With the breeze gone even wisps of dust blowing down the street were gone. It all looked like a still life, unreal and placid. Looking at the hills ahead of them his sense of foreboding grew stronger over what they might find on the other side.

Antonio is aware that it won't be the same but just how different was his concern. He also felt the chances of finding anyone much less his family were getting slimmer by the moment. It hurt. He didn't want it that way, but maybe Pat was right on that score. They've found no one else anywhere they've traveled, not on any road, town, city street, or in any building between Dublin and Sacramento. Why should they find Maria now? What were the realistic chances of finding anyone now?

He hated these long drives, even before all this started. It always gives him time to think, usually about things he'd rather not think about. He can't turn on the radio as there are no DJ's to listen to anymore. No radio stations broadcasting news, weather, sports, or music. He didn't miss the radio talk shows. He listened to a couple of them some years ago and all he got out of it was stupid people calling in to talk to stupid hosts who thought they knew more than anybody else about everything. As far as Antonio was concerned, they knew a lot less than they thought they did. Even if somebody was on the air now, would anybody be calling in? The thought occurred to him to try the radio again but it just as fleetingly left him. It would only mean another disappointment.

Heading into the Altamont Pass Pat grew less restive and even cracked half a smile. He was approaching more familiar territory which of course made him feel more comfortable. The stress of all that happened since early this morning had really taken its toll on him. He knew it but couldn't help it. He never had the ability to handle traumatic situations and for years relied on Antonio to pull him through tough times. From high school and through the years the few relationships that did last more than a weekend, it was always Antonio who helped him keep his sanity. Even now here in their present dilemma he knew he will need to lean on Antonio to make it through. He didn't always agree with Antonio, but he knew he could rely on him as a friend and a support when needed. For now, Pat decided he was going to play it by ear and see where things go from here.

As they make the final curve in the road that brought the first view of the tri-valley floor before them they both stared intensely at the sight below. A blanket of smoke covered the valley like a dark layer of high fog. Pockets of flame were still visible, but smoke and ash rose from fewer locations than either of them had expected.

Not long after they left the area this morning the wind started dying down and the spread of flames from existing fires slowed considerably. Many thoughts raced through both their minds as they approached Livermore's eastern edge. Antonio was torn between slowing down to take it all in mentally recapping all that transpired since early this morning, and speeding up to reach home and resume his too long delayed search for Maria and the kids. He floored the accelerator weaving in and out of the stranded and vacant vehicles frequently using the shoulder of the freeway to pass more congested sections.

Pat wasn't sure why Antonio suddenly increased speed but didn't ask any questions as he was happy to be getting home quickly. Home he thought. Just what does that mean? Home was always a place to eat, sleep, watch TV, and have sex when he was lucky. He only now realizes that home had an entirely different meaning to Antonio. A wife, kids, a family made a house a home, not the location. Pat has begun to understand what he has been missing and what he never understood how to obtain, actually feared to obtain. Even now the thought of family brings conflicting feelings of fear and desire. His fear now is the opportunity to find a truly meaningful and positive relationship that might have given him a chance of a family of his own will never happen. He wasn't sure whether to cry or be grateful.

They were approaching the first Dublin off ramp. Smoke still rose from several buildings around town, but they couldn't see any real flames from the freeway. There were signs of burnt out sections of business parks and strip malls. Some homes in residential areas were burned down to the ground. A few buildings had small burned sections that for whatever reason failed to take, leaving the question, "did it really go out by itself, or did someone put it out?" Most likely sprinkler systems helped keep some fires from completely destroying a few commercial buildings.

Antonio turned to Pat and cautiously asked, "Maybe we should get off here and just start a street by street search pattern across town? We already hit the most obvious places they might be before we left this morning."

"That was over eight hours ago. If those were the most likely places then maybe we should hit them again real quick just to be sure they didn't go there after we left," Pat suggested.

Antonio was pleasantly surprised at the obvious logic of Pat's suggestion. "That's the best thing you said all day. Let's do it." Antonio sped up to the Dougherty off ramp and headed into Dublin to his apartment. They passed the sports grounds on the way. The playground and sports fields were empty. Along the way they could see the sporadic patterns in the burned out buildings created by the wind before it died down. As they passed one building with only a small burned section of roof Antonio slowed down. They saw no signs of attempts to put out the fire. There were no hoses or portable extinguishers lying nearby. Their only conclusion was sprinkler systems and, or fire retardant materials were used in the building construction. They didn't stop to verify their thoughts as they were still on a mission of greater importance.

As they turned onto the street where Antonio lived they slowed to a crawl as their hearts sank. The entire apartment complex was burned to the ground.

Chapter 25

Antonio pulled up to the curb near what used to be the entrance to his apartment. They got out and stood on the sidewalk staring at the sight before them. Smoke still rose from a number of hot spots throughout the burned out hulk of what used to be home. Recognizable sections like a stairway on their far left stood up out of the rubble like a beacon to futility. With no one around to fight the flames all was consumed by the roaring conflagration that ran through the complex. Nowhere was there anything one could rummage through in an effort to find surviving keepsakes, no photos, no trophies, no wall mounted certificates celebrating higher achievements, no souvenirs from last summer's vacation, no letters, diaries, newspaper clippings highlighting the kids activities at school or in scouts, nothing.

It hit Antonio hard. He fell back against the car feeling helpless and hopeless. Now not only was his family gone, but so was anything that proved they ever existed. Pictures in his wallet were all that was left of his family. His only thought now, "Lord, I hope they weren't there."

Pat looked away and also thought out loud, "Don't worry, I don't think any body was in there."

"This time I hope you're right. Let's get over to Murray School," he said, his voice now reflecting the conclusion their search is without any real hope of finding anyone. He finally accepts the probable fact that his family has gone wherever everyone else has gone, wherever that is. Antonio went back around to the driver's side and got in. He started the engine and turned to wait for Pat to get in. Pat was slowly scanning the neighborhood when he looked in the direction of Antonio's stare. He turned back to the car and jumped in, "Sorry. I just couldn't help but see what's happened around us. Nothing is the same and it never will be. I don't care what we find or don't find. Nothing will ever be the same."

Amazing thought Antonio. That's twice now in less than ten minutes we agree on something. Maybe we are getting back in sync. He gunned the engine and peeled out from the curb heading for the kids school. It wasn't far and they were there in quick order. The school was intact and sitting in silent tribute to the education of a society that no longer existed. A late evening breeze was starting to kick in picking up small dust swirls in the yard and moving the empty hanging swings in the deserted play ground.

Antonio remembers when the school was in session the yard filled with running screaming kids having fun playing kick ball, hanging from the monkey bars, swinging on the swings, or floating down the slides. He can remember the few times he brought the kids here on weekends or summer days just to play on the playground or play catch with Ryan. He now fears those days are gone for good, that the chance of playing catch with Ryan or pushing Theresa on the swing will never happen again, but he still doesn't understand why.

"We could check the classrooms if you want, but I think you know what we'll find," said Pat.

Antonio sighed, "Yea, I know, but I have to be sure." He headed for the hall where Theresa's classroom was located. Opening the door to the hallway created an echolike hollow empty sound he never noticed before. All he could think was the comments they made earlier how nothing would ever be the same again. The emptiness reinforced that feeling. The feeling is growing now that the likelihood of finding his family, or anyone else, is gone. It's not how he wants to feel but the evidence is overwhelming.

Theresa's classroom is empty as is Ryan's. They check the office and the faculty lounge with the same result. Antonio walked slowly out to the parking lot in silence. Pat caught up with him, "You still want to go over to the park?"

"Yea, let's go."

"I hope you're not serious about a street by street search. It would take too much time and you know it won't do any good." Pat wasn't sure how Antonio would react but he just couldn't see wasting all that time on something so futile. They're not going to find anyone. Antonio was quiet on the way to the car. They got in. Antonio started the engine and turned to Pat.

"You may be right, but there has to be some way we can determine if anyone is still around, some way to just be sure." He drove over to the park where they spent some time earlier this morning on the same mission. It was empty as expected. They sat parked next to the curb in silence. Pat had no clue as to what to do or where to go next. His only thought at this point was to decide on how best to survive.

Antonio was thinking how best to be sure he'd done everything possible to find his family before giving up on the search. He wanted to be of clear conscience before going on with what might be left of their lonely existence, though feelings that what was left was about to come to an end still haunt him. The feelings that a conclusion or an answer was coming still hung there in the back of his thoughts just as the feelings months ago began making him wonder if he was losing his mind. He constantly looked around for something different or new or out of place with the new order of things hoping to find a clue as to what was coming. There was nothing. Maybe it would come in its own good time just like everything else.

Pat finally broke the silence, "Alright, where from here? Any ideas?"

"Yea, let's go to the top of snob hill. From there we can see over all of Dublin and San Ramon. We use the binoculars and try to locate any sign of life, any movement not related to the wind. If we don't find anything at that point I concede the possibility that no one is left. That doesn't mean they aren't, just the possibility. From there we'll just go on with what we have to do to get by."

"We have the start a plan," was all Pat could say, but he was happy to hear what Antonio said.

Pat was relieved to get on with the necessities of survival but he did feel for his friend. He reached to the back seat searching for the binoculars while Antonio pulled away from the curb heading west toward snob hill. As they climbed the road through one of Dublin's better neighborhoods they were struck by the vanity of a society that found value in climbing the social ladder, that material possessions carried a built in path to happiness that was equal to carrying a heart filled with love and caring about family in particular, and humanity at large.

Antonio wondered if the human race was being punished for their misplaced priorities, or was this a totally random cosmic event. While he struggled to find a reason for their predicament, he found the latter alternative hard to accept. That would mean life really had no purpose or meaning, and he found that unbearable. And this whole line of thought still brought him back to the main question of the day, why was it that he and Pat were the only ones left? What possible meaning or purpose could that have regarding anything?

Not for the first time Antonio mentally kicked himself, "Stop thinking, stupid. You just get yourself into trouble!" He looked at his friend and concluded Pat also was deeper into thought than was his usual habit.

Pat knew that no matter where they decided to go it would be necessary to stock up on basic needs, food, water, proper clothing, etc. They still had a few of the supplies they picked up this morning at the sporting goods store. They would need to replace the gear left behind if they were to head for the hills. That was his preference, get away from the empty hollow feeling left by the remains of a civilization lost. Of course there was something to be said for staying, shelter, food supply, some conveniences of modern society that survived. But these things would give out sooner or later and better to get used to foraging for your continued existence right from the start was Pat's strong gut feeling.

Pat didn't know how Antonio would feel about it but he would convince his friend to leave all this behind. It might be better to leave all that reminded him of what he's lost. The constant visual reminders of his family, where they lived, played, worked, could put Antonio in a constant depression. What Pat failed to recognize is the fact that some people could find the familiar surroundings comforting. How Antonio would handle it was too early to tell. It could be a double edged sword, maybe a comfortable depression.

Pat was now beginning to feel he was thinking too much. This wasn't like him either. Deep thought wasn't his cup of tea. He usually left the thinking to Antonio. Pat was more comfortable simply reacting to situations and worry about the consequences later. Pat snapped out of his line of thought with Antonio's abrupt right turn onto the ridge top drive where the view of the whole Dublin, San Ramon area spread out below.

Under normal and more pleasant times of the recent past, the view could be breath taking and beautiful. Antonio remembered several occasions when he and Maria would bring the kids up here just to see the view. They would park along the road and get out for a stroll along the ridge. The kids loved to find and point out their school, their friend's homes, and other points of individual interest to each of them. One fourth of July they even came up here to watch the fire works, those from the formal shows put on at several valley locations, and the hundreds of neighborhood displays on every street in the area. It was quite impressive and the kids loved it, but it meant not shooting off their own fire works in front of their own apartment. The next year it was a tough decision for the kids to decide which to do, but they decided to stay home and do their own fire works. But they were glad to have seen the view from on top at least once.

While the pain of remembering the good times still hurt as much as ever, Antonio found he was handling it better. He scanned the view from left to right looking for any sign of life, or anything close to it. Pat was doing the same. Smoke still rose from several locations, though the intensity of it was much reduced. Some burned out areas still smoldered but it appeared the fires were dying down and any further threat in that regard was disappearing.

The smoke was heading east indicating a light breeze from over the hill at their backs was blowing the smoke away from them. This helped keep the view of the area below clear as much as could be expected under the circumstances. Using their binoculars they continued to scan the valley below looking for any sign that they were not alone. Occasionally they saw light debris blowing across the open streets but nothing in the way of movement that could not be attributed to the wind. Nowhere was there even the slightest hint of any living creature, large or small, two legged or four, walking, crawling, or flying.

The sun was now below the line of the hill behind them and dusk was setting in. It would still be light for about an hour. Pat was satisfied that there wasn't any sign of life and was ready to quit. Antonio continued to search. He knew now it was futile, but he had to be sure. He wanted to be clear of conscience that he did everything possible to find them. He looked at every possible place they might have gone. He looked again and again till even he had to admit there is no one left in the area. At least no one was venturing outside. Could they be hold up inside somewhere hiding from whatever evil seemed to be lurking outside? It was a possibility, but even Antonio had to admit a very remote one.

He sighed with a heavy heart and brought his binoculars down from his eyes. He looked at Pat. "It seems we've come the end of our search. I concede we have to go on. Oh, I'll keep looking, but I admit we now have concentrate on moving forward. Let's find a place to stay tonight and tomorrow we can make some choices. I'm too tired to think about it tonight."

"I'm with you on that. Sorry about everything, man. I wish we could have found them," said Pat.

"Don't apologize. It's not your fault," replied Antonio as he turned back to the car.

Pat gestured with his arm sweeping the view below, "Where would you like to stay, we have plenty of places to choose from?"

Antonio looked out over the house tops, "Not in somebody's house. It just wouldn't feel right. The Holiday Inn is open. They must have a couple of suites available. Let's check it out."

Pat chuckled, "I don't know man. We didn't make any reservations. You're pushing it."

"I'd love to find somebody there, but some how I doubt we will," said Antonio.

"Damn," complained Pat. "That means no room service."

"You idiot," shouted Antonio.

"Up yours," replied Pat.

Antonio realized things were starting to get back to normal between them. It wasn't quite there yet but it was going in the right direction. That should be a good sign. So why was he feeling that something wasn't right. It was that old feeling that started months ago, that something was out of kilter. Things were not what they seemed. The odd premonition that something was about to happen that he experienced months ago was hanging in there again. He didn't know what it meant then and he doesn't know what it means now. He only knows it can't be good, not based on what this day has been like. How much worse can it get he thought? He didn't want to know the answer to that one.

Unfortunately he was afraid he was going to find out sooner than he wanted to. The problem now as they drove to the hotel was shall he tell Pat about his feelings? He knows he made a promise to Pat that he would fill him in on any more premonitions or feelings. Their relationship has started to get back toward normal and he was afraid to jeopardize that. How would informing Pat affect their current situation? Antonio decided to hold off for now. Maybe tomorrow would be better.

They approached the hotel. Walking into the lobby they looked around. The front desk was on the left. They brought in the camping lanterns thinking the power was out. Much to their pleasant surprise the power was still on.

"Look for a master key," Antonio instructed Pat.

"Right," said Pat as he ran behind the desk and started searching. "I think I've found it," he said raising a key card over his head. They took the elevator to the top floor and searched the best rooms for something they each liked and made themselves at home. They showered and cleaned up. Both agreed that a good night's sleep would help them with clearer heads in the morning. They could discuss their future over breakfast.

Antonio went back to his room of choice and went to bed. Thoughts of Maria kept him from drifting of to sleep right away, but his sheer exhaustion brought on by the days events had him out before long.

In his room of choice Pat turned on the TV out of habit. The hotel had an in house library of movies he could select from using the remote control in his room. He found something a bit soft porn and put it on. He lay down on the couch and went sleep before the first actress had her clothes off.

Chapter 26

The night was quiet, quieter than man has known since the creation of the world. There were no sounds of crickets chirping, no night owls hooting, no frogs croaking, no cats fighting, no dogs howling. There was no traffic noise from the freeway close by, no horns honking on the local streets, no music from the corner bar, no patrons arguing, and no sirens in the night, no loud party noise from an obnoxious neighbor. There was nothing but the silence of the new world where the only sounds came from the light breeze outside and the snoring in two rooms of the Holiday Inn where the worlds last two inhabitants rested.

The two inhabitants dreamed in their sleep. Their dreams have common themes yet are quite different. They both looked back on what once was, one with heartache and happiness, the other on what might have been in a better world. They are filled with those who meant the most and were a great part in shaping who they became. We are all shaped by those who influence our lives; the good, the bad, and the indifferent. The example shown by those around us helps shape our future and influence the choices we make. We observe the good in those we love and can choose to follow their example. The same can be said for the wrong we see in them. We can choose to follow or reject that also. Even the indifference shown by others with regard to things like hate and prejudice, pain and suffering of others, can influence our own attitudes about the world around us and those who inhabit it. The choice however, in the direction we follow, is still our own. We still have the freedom to choose our own values and course of action, or we can choose to be silent, uncaring, and indifferent.

Antonio dreamed of the first time he met Maria, their first date, their first kiss, their wedding night. He dreamed of the birth of Theresa and Ryan, their first steps, first words, first days of school. He dreamed of the good times, days together at the beach or at the movies. He didn't want to wake up. This is what made life worth living. It's what gave meaning and purpose to his existence.

Pat also dreamed of his family. He dreamed of what he missed. He dreamed of a childhood filled with the love of parents who showed they cared, who took an interest in the things he did and activities he was involved in. It wasn't just Uncle Mike who took him camping and fishing. His parents were there also. His dad and uncle were both there coaching his little league team. It was all he had ever wanted and longed for, but never knew. He didn't want to wake up either. He never knew this kind of happiness in the real world. But he had dreamed of it, wished for it, begged God for it. When it never came he lost his faith, not only in God, but in people and in living. Only Uncle Mike and the friendship of Antonio and Maria kept him sane.

The sun rose slowly in the east. The day promised to be cooler than yesterday. A light breeze still filled the air. Much of the smoke had dissipated leaving only enough to color the air with a golden haze and an unpleasant odor of charred wood and other less pleasant odors of burned and melted man made materials. Antonio's room had an eastern facing window and even with the heavy dark curtains blocking the light enough shown through to cause him to stir. It was a slow and restless awakening.

His dreams were too good to give up and he would be content to continue to dream them for days to come, maybe longer. It was better than the reality to which he was waking. He rolled over onto his stomach and groaned. He didn't know what this day would bring but he was already feeling that this day would point the direction of their future in more ways than one. He couldn't explain it. The feeling was strong that today was pivotal. One way or another, this was it. He got up slowly and dressed. The unknown has always made him apprehensive. He liked things planned out, predictable. Not knowing what was ahead made him nervous. He was nervous now.

Pat woke up, not so much because of the light, but more because his dreams had come to an end. He was back to reality. While he was disappointed to end the dreams he had longed for, he was satisfied that he had them at last. His only sorrow was that these dreams had never been the reality he missed. He decided that he wasn't going to feel sorry for himself anymore. He'd done that for too long. He still had the best friend he had ever known beside him during these tough times and whatever future lay ahead for them his friend would still be there. Only Uncle Mike would have been a better companion with what the future may hold. It was time to get up and get on with it. He dressed in a hurry and left the room to join Antonio in making whatever decisions had to be made regarding the future they had in store.

Pat started to knock on the door to Antonio's room when the door opened. They stared at each other for a second each a little surprised at how well rested the other appeared.

"Come in," offered Antonio. Pat walked in stepping over a pile of clothes and other paraphernalia left behind by the residents of the room before the great disappearing act. Antonio walked over to the kitchenette and opened the refrigerator. They were surprised to see some eggs and a pound of bacon, sausage, on the shelf among a few other basic breakfast staples. "Damn, no potatoes."

"Check the freeze compartment," suggested Pat.

Antonio opened the door to the small freezer compartment and found a small package of frozen hash browns and some popsicles. "Well I'll be damned. It may not be fresh but under the circumstances I'll take it." He grabbed the hash browns and tossed them on the counter by the stove. The bacon, sausage, and eggs were next. Antonio made their breakfast while Pat stared out the window at their new world. He still believed the best plan for the future lay in leaving the area for the hills where there was plenty of game and wide open spaces to live in. Our forefathers did it. There was no reason they couldn't. It hit him like a lightening bolt. GAME! What game? There is no game anymore.

"Oh, my god," he said aloud.

Antonio turned startled. "You see something?"

"No. I just realized my whole set of plans for the future won't exactly work the way I planned. I figured we could hunt for game, grow our own veggies, the whole bit. But there is no game, not if what we've seen so far is any example. Unless things are different up in the hills, there won't be any game to hunt. Damn, I never wanted to be a vegetarian."

Antonio saw a dejected look in Pat's face. He didn't want to start a discussion about the future just yet. He wasn't sure there will be a future. "Let's eat first, and then we can talk about what we're going to do, alright? Sit down. It's almost ready."

"Sure." Pat walked over to the table and sat opposite Antonio. Breakfast was eaten in silence. They were each lost in their own thoughts about what the new day in the new world would bring. Pat was disillusioned over what he hoped would be their future roaming the hills hunting game and living off the land. It hadn't occurred to him until now that without a sign of any other living creatures, there wasn't anything to hunt. He would have to rethink his entire line of reasoning as to where their future would lie. He would have to listen more closely to what ideas Antonio had in mind. Even if he didn't like Antonio's ideas, they might give him some new hints as to where to go from here.

When Antonio finished he pushed his plate towards Pat, "Your turn to do the dishes."

"Shit. Let the maid do it."

"There is no maid dummy," Antonio laughed. They chuckled and shook their heads. It was quiet for a moment. Then Pat broke the silence.

"O.K. What now?"

"I don't know. There's food and water here, at least for a while. The canned food in the stores should last for years, the same for bottled water. We can get gas to run generators for electricity when the power does go out. We can watch all the videos we want. I'm sure the video stores no longer have a short return policy."

Pat laughed at that. "You got that right. I guess it's not so bad here for now, at least for a while. Sooner or later we may get tired of the same routine. We may want to see what else is out there. Even if we don't see anyone we could see the places we never visited before but always wanted to see."

"Without Maria I doubt that would interest me any more. Maybe in time," Antonio added quickly seeing the look on Pat's face. "This isn't a bad place to hold up for awhile."

"We can start collecting the supplies we need from the local stores and store them in the lobby or stock room somewhere down stairs," suggested Pat.

"We can start storing gasoline in cans somewhere near by. Once the power goes the pumps won't work. Once that's gone we'll be on foot. Too bad we couldn't find some horses," replied Antonio.

"Maybe we could take a trip out to the country and see if there are some cows or horses still around," thought Pat aloud.

"If we didn't see any on our way to Sacramento and back I seriously doubt we'll find any now," Antonio reminded him.

"Damn, I know you're right. It was just wishful thinking."

"At least you're thinking," smirked Antonio.

"Up yours."

"You know what I miss right now," asked Antonio?

"What's that?"

"The morning paper."

"Why? All they ever reported was bad news. You know, like the end of the world, stuff like that," replied Pat.

"I still miss the sports page and the comics. I guess there's no more of that," Antonio mused.

"Now that you mention it, you know we'll have to keep ourselves busy. I mean like with exercise and stuff."

Antonio looked at Pat, "You mean like find a gym?"

"Yea, that, or we can find some sports activities like bowling, tennis, one on one basketball, you know, stuff like that."

"I've always wanted to take up golf."

"Golf! You got to be kidding. I can't think of anything more boring. It shouldn't even be considered a sport. It's just for lazy old rich men with nothing better to do. Golf, what a joke," Pat spewed.

"O.K. We can skip the golf. I think we ought to make a survey today of the local stores still standing where we can start raiding for supplies. Get an idea of what's still around and available. We need to start getting organized," Antonio pointed out.

Pat thought a minute, "You know, I remember seeing a truck parked on the side of the building when we came in last night. It might work for transporting our supplies from the stores to here."

"Well, we don't need to start bringing things in right away. The truck will come in handy, but for now, let's just survey the area for what's still standing and useful, not burned out. We can make a list of what's available where, and plan a schedule for getting our supplies. What do you think?"

"Sounds like a plan to me. You want to get started now," asked Pat.

"As good a time as any. Let's go," stated Antonio.

They headed out of the parking lot for the main shopping areas of Dublin. Thirty to forty percent of some blocks were burned out while others remained relatively in tact. Mervyn's was still there and they marked it available for clothing. The sporting goods store in the Gemco shopping center was in good shape. They went by the Lucky's grocery store where they picked up supplies earlier, but it was gone. Gutted out by a fire that was started in the restaurant next door.

While driving around checking the stores and making their list, Antonio kept feeling he was really wasting his time. There is no need for the list as there won't be any need for the supplies. The feeling was getting stronger now that this was it. Today would be the end of it all. All of what? He didn't know. He couldn't explain it now any more than he could several months ago. He was still torn as to whether or not he should tell Pat about his feelings.

He knows he promised no more secrets, no more holding back about his premonitions, but he just couldn't bring himself to fill Pat in on his feelings yet. On what? That's the problem. How do you explain something to someone when you can't even explain it to yourself? You can't, or at least he can't. Not yet. I need a little more time thought Antonio.

Pat was unaware of the mental turmoil his friend was going through and was concentrating on the job at hand. He turned to Antonio, "Let's try the Albertson's over by the freeway. Isn't that where Maria did her shopping?"

"Yea, good idea," said Antonio. The mention of Maria's name gave him a pang of guilt about giving up on the search for her and the kids, but he even thought maybe they were in the store. After all, there was plenty of food and drinks. Why not? He knew it was wishful thinking on his part, but while he may have given up on an active search, he was still keeping an open eye for the possibility he might see them somewhere by chance. He wasn't giving up completely. After all, even his premonitions could be wrong. Actually, he hoped that was the case.

They turned right onto Foothill Boulevard and headed toward the Albertson's shopping center on the northwest end of town. Along the way they passed St. Raymond's Catholic Church on the left. It brought many memories back to Antonio. He slowed down as they passed the church. The turn going up the hill approached.

"What are you doing?" asked Pat.

"I need to make a stop," said Antonio matter-of-factly without explaining. He turned up to the church and pulled into the parking lot in front of the entrance. He got out and turned to Pat saying, "I won't take long. You can come in or wait here if you like."

"I'll just wait here. You go ahead. Take whatever time you need," said Pat. He wasn't a praying man himself although lately he has begun to wonder if that was something he might need to change.

Antonio headed for the church. He went in placing his right fingers in the holy water and crossing himself. He headed down the aisle about half way, genuflected and slipped into a pew; he kneeled and began to pray. He prayed for Maria and the kids. He prayed for Pat and himself in their present situation. He prayed for some understanding about what was happening and why. He also asked God for a resolution one way or another regarding their present situation. It was necessary to rid himself of these damn feelings and premonitions of impending doom. One way or another he had to know and he wanted to either join the others wherever they were, or get on with the rest of his life without worrying about weird noises or strange goings on. He continued to pray as he never prayed in his life. He poured out his heart trying to rid himself of any guilt he felt about the loss of his family, and for some understanding.

He doesn't know how long he was there. When he stood he knew it was longer than he anticipated or realized. He wanted to get out to the car before Pat decided to leave without him. As he approached the car he realized something was wrong. The doors to the car were closed but it appeared to be empty. Where was Pat? He looked into the car to be sure Pat wasn't just slumped inside asleep. He wasn't there. Antonio looked up and around his heart racing. Had Pat gotten impatient and left, after all Antonio had the keys. No, if Pat got impatient he would have come inside and get Antonio to hurry up.

Antonio looked around the parking lot. It was empty. He walked first to one side of the building than to the other and could not see Pat anywhere. He called Pat's name over and over until he was shouting at the top of his lungs. No answer. His voice just echoed in the wind. Antonio opened every unlocked door he could find, from the parish office to the Rectory, and the school classrooms. He double checked the church, the small chapel on the north side, and the crying room where parents with unruly or restless kids could still observe mass. It slowly came to him that maybe Pat was gone now too, and that he was completely alone. Fear gripped him like never before.

It was one thing to be one of the last two people left on earth. Certainly that was how it seemed. But to be the only one left with no one to talk to, no one to share the pain and endure the living with under these unique circumstances would be unbearable. Antonio spent about half an hour searching the church grounds and other buildings before he finally came to the conclusion that this was it. He was actually alone. Is this the it he had been questioning all morning? Is that what he has been expecting, that he would be left alone now forever? Why? Why him and not Pat? Why him and not any body else? Who the hell was he? He wanted some answers. He looked back at the church.

Antonio walked slowly back into the church without crossing himself with the holy water. He walked up the aisle to the front of the church and approached the altar. He stared up at the risen Christ on the cross hanging above the altar not sure what to do now or what to think. He knelt. Antonio was more confused now than ever. He prayed.

The inside of the church began to fill with a bright light. It seemed to fill the air and encompass everything in a blanket of angelic warmth. A strange noise filled the air, what a beautiful noise it was. It sounded like the beautiful voices of angels singing. It filled him and surrounded him. Antonio was happier than he had ever known. Then there was silence, the total silence of an empty world.

www.ingramcontent.com/pod-product-compliance
Lightning Source LLC
Chambersburg PA
CBHW030819310726
48980CB00006B/550/J

* 9 7 8 0 6 1 5 1 3 6 4 4 8 *